Mary Emmeline Manners

The Bishop and the Caterpillar

as recited by Mr. Brandram - and other pieces

Mary Emmeline Manners

The Bishop and the Caterpillar
as recited by Mr. Brandram - and other pieces

ISBN/EAN: 9783337406004

Printed in Europe, USA, Canada, Australia, Japan

Cover: Foto ©Andreas Hilbeck / pixelio.de

More available books at **www.hansebooks.com**

THE BISHOP AND THE CATERPILLAR

AND OTHER PIECES.

THE BISHOP AND THE CATERPILLAR

(As Recited by Mr. Brandram)

AND OTHER PIECES

BY

MARY E. MANNERS

London:

JAMES CLARKE & CO., 13 & 14, FLEET STREET.

—

1892.

Dedicated

TO

LEWIS CARROL,

IN GRATEFUL REMEMBRANCE

OF MANY HAPPY HOURS

SPENT IN

" WONDERLAND."

Carrol! Accept the heartfelt thanks
  Of children of all ages,
Of those who long have left their ranks,
  Yet still must love the pages
Written by him whose magic wand
Called up the scenes of " Wonderland."

PREFACE.

~~~~~~~~~

THE whole of these poems, with the exception of
the last four, will be familiar to the readers of
The Boy's Own Paper,* having appeared at intervals
in the pages of that periodical, from which they
are now reprinted by special permission. The
exceptions have been collected from various sources,
and several have made their *début* at the social
gatherings of an Essay Meeting composed of
members of the "Society of Friends," whose kindly
appreciation first encouraged me to hope that the
pieces might be found suitable for reading and
recitation by a wider circle of friends (with or
without the capital " F "). " The Bishop and the

---

* *The Boy's Own Paper*, which was started by the Religious Tract
Society, 56, Paternoster Row, to provide high-class literature for
boys, has long been quite a household word in every part of the
English-speaking world.

Caterpillar" has, I understand, been largely used for this purpose.

For the rest, my enjoyment of the mysterious title of "Anon" has been almost equal to Mark Tapley's wonder at finding himself transformed into a " Co."; but I am told that this dignity is no longer a desirable one; so it is with even greater pleasure that I subscribe myself to all who are interested in the matter as

Their sincere well-wisher,

MARY E. MANNERS.

CONTENTS.

THE BISHOP AND THE CATERPILLAR.

~~~~~~~~~~~~~~~~~~~

THE Bishop sat in the Schoolmaster's chair :
The Rector, and Curates two, were there,
    The Doctor, the Squire,
    The heads of the Choir,
And the Gentry around of high degree,
A highly distinguished company ;
For the Bishop was greatly beloved in his See !

    And there, below,
    A goodly show,
Their faces with soap and with pleasure aglow,
Sat the dear little school-children, row upon row ;
For the Bishop had said ('twas the death-blow to
    schism),
He would hear those dear children their Catechism.
    And then to complete
    The pleasure so sweet

1

Of these nice little children so pretty and neat,
He'd invited them to a magnificent treat!
And filled were the minds of these dear little ones
With visions of cakes, and of "gay Sally Lunns,"
Of oceans of tea, and unlimited buns
(The large ones called "Bath," not the plain penny
    ones).

      I think I have read,
      Or at least heard it said:
"Boys are always in mischief, unless they're in bed."
      I put it to you,
      I don't say it's true,
But if you should ask for my own private view,
I should answer at once, without further ado:
"I don't think a boy can be trusted to keep
From mischief in bed—unless he's asleep!"

But the Schoolmaster's eye hath a magic spell,
And the boys were behaving remarkably well—
For boys; and the girls—but 'tis needless to say
Their conduct was perfect in every way;
For I'm sure 'tis well known in all ranks of society,
That girls *always* behave with the utmost propriety.

Now the Bishop arises, and waves his hand;
And the children prepared for his questions stand;

With admiring eyes his form they scan ;
He was a remarkably fine-looking man !
His apron was silk of the blackest dye,
His lawn the finest money could buy ;
His sleeves and his ruffles than snow were whiter,
He'd his best shovel-hat, and his second-best
mitre.
With benignant glance he gazed around—
You might have heard the slightest sound !—
With dignified mien and solemn look
He slowly opened his ponderous book,
And proceeded at once the knowledge to try
Of those nice little children standing by.

Each child knew its name,
And who gave it the same,
And all the rest of the questions profound
Which his Lordship was pleased to the school to
propound.
Nor less did secular knowledge abound,
For the Bishop, to his great pleasure, found
That they knew the date when our Queen was
crowned,
And the number of pence which make up a pound ;
And the oceans and seas which our island bound ;
That the earth is nearly, but not quite, round ;
Their orthography, also, was equally sound,

And the Bishop, at last, completely astound-
      Ed, cried,
      In a tone of pride,
"You bright little dears, no question can trouble you,
You've spelled knife with a *k*, and wrong with a *w*.

"And now that my pleasing task's at an end,
I trust you will make of me a friend :
You've answered my questions, and 'tis but fair
That I in replying should take a share ;
So if there is aught you would like to know,
Pray ask me about it before I go.
I'm sure it would give me the greatest pleasure
To add to your knowledge, for learning's a treasure
Which you never can lose, and which no one can
    steal ;
It grows by imparting, so do not feel
      Afraid or shy,
      But boldly try,
    Which is the cleverer, you or I ! "
Thus amusement with learning judiciously blending,
His Lordship made of his speech an ending,
And a murmur went round of " How condescend-
    ing ! "

But one bright little boy didn't care a jot
If his Lordship were condescending or not ;

For, with scarce a pause
For the sounds of applause,
He raised his head,
And abruptly said :
" How many legs has a Caterpillar got ? "

Now the Bishop was a learned man,
Bishops always were since the race began,
But his knowledge in that particular line
Was less than yours, and no greater than mine ;
And, except that he knew the creature could crawl,
He knew nothing about its legs at all—
Whether the number were great or small,
One hundred, or five, or sixty, or six,—
So he felt in a "pretty consid'rable fix ! "
But, resolving his ignorance to hide,
In measured tones he thus replied :

" The Caterpillar, my dear little boy,
Is an emblem of life and a vision of joy !
It bursts from its shell on a bright green leaf,
It knows no care and it feels no grief."
Then he turned to the Rector and whispered low,
" Mr. Rector, how many ? You surely must know."
But the Rector gravely shook his head,
He hadn't the faintest idea, he said.
So the Bishop turned to the class again,
And in tones paternal took up the strain :

" The Caterpillar, dear children, see,
On its bright green leaf from care lives free,
And it eats, and eats, and grows bigger and bigger,
(Perhaps the Curates can state the figure ?) "
But the Curates couldn't ; the Bishop went on,
Though he felt that another chance was gone.

"So it eats, and eats, and it grows and grows,
(Just ask the Schoolmaster if he knows.)"
But the Schoolmaster said that that kind of know-
    ledge
Was not the sort he had learned at college.
" And when it has eaten enough, then soon
It spins for itself a soft cocoon,
And then it becomes a chrysalis—
I wonder which child can spell me this ?
'Tis rather a difficult word to spell—
(Just ask the Schoolmistress if she can tell.) "
But the Schoolmistress said, as she shook her grey
    curls,
"She considered such things were not proper for
    girls."

The word was spelled, and spelled quite right,
Those nice little boys were so awfully bright !
And the Bishop began to get into a fright,
His face grew red—it was formerly white—

And the hair on his head stood nearly upright;
He was almost inclined to take refuge in flight,
But he thought that would be too shocking a sight;
He was at his wits' end—nearly—not quite,
For the Pupil Teachers caught his eye.
He thought they might know—at least he would
    try—
Then he anxiously waited for their reply:
But the Pupil Teachers enjoyed the fun,
And they wouldn't have told if they could have done.

So he said to the Beadle, "Go down in the street,
And stop all the people you chance to meet,
      I don't care who,
      Any one will do;
The old woman selling lollipops,
The little boys playing with marbles and tops,
Or respectable people who deal at the shops;
The crossing-sweeper, the organ-grinder,
Or the fortune-teller, if you can find her.
      Ask any or all,
      Short or tall,
    Great or small, it matters not—
How many legs has a Caterpillar got?"
The Beadle bowed, and was off like a shot
From a pop-gun fired, or that classical arrow
Which flew from the bow of the wicked cock-sparrow.

Now the Bishop again put on a smile,
And the children, who had been waiting meanwhile,
In their innocent hearts imagined that these
      Remarks applied
      (They were spoken aside)
To the weighty affairs of the Diocese.

" The Caterpillar is doomed to sleep
For months—a slumber long and deep.
      Brown and dead
      It looks, 'tis said,
It never even requires to be fed ;
And, except that sometimes it waggles its head,
Your utmost efforts would surely fail
To distinguish the creature's head from its tail.

  " But one morning in spring,
    When the birds loudly sing,
And the earth is gay with blossoming ;
    When the violets blue
    Are wet with dew,
And the sky wears the sweetest cerulean hue !
    When on all is seen
    The brightest sheen—
When the daisies are white, and the grass is green ;
    Then the chrysalis breaks,
    The insect awakes,—

To the realms of air its way it takes ;
    It did not die,
    It soars on high,
A bright and a beauteous butterfly ! "

Here he paused and wiped a tear from his eye ;
The Beadle was quietly standing by,
And perceiving the lecture had reached its close,
Whispered, softly and sadly, " Nobody knows ! "

The Bishop saw his last hope was vain,
But to make the best of it he was fain ;
So he added, " Dear children, we ever should be
Prepared to learn from all we see,
And beautiful thoughts of hope and joy
Fill the heart, I know, of each girl and boy !
Oh, ponder on these, and you will not care
To know the exact allotted share
Of *legs* the creature possessed at its birth,
When it crawled, a mean worm, on this lowly earth.
Yet, if you know it, you now may tell,
Your answers so far have pleased me well."

Then he looked around with benignant eye,
Nor long did he wait for the reply,
For the bright little boy, with a countenance gay,
Said, " Six, for I counted 'em yesterday ! "

MORAL.

" To all who have children under their care,"
Of two things, nay, three things, I pray you beware—
Don't give them too many " unlimited buns,"
Six each (Bath) is sufficient, or twelve penny ones ;
Don't let them go in for examination,
Unless you have given them due preparation,
Or the questions, asked with the kindest intention,
May be rather a strain on their powers of invention.
Don't pretend you know everything under the sun,
Though your school-days are ended, and theirs but
    begun,
But honestly say, when the case is so,
" This thing, my dear children, I do not know ; "
For they really must learn, either slower or speedier
That you're not a walking Encyclopædia !

A HOLIDAY STORY FOR BOYS
—AND THEIR UNCLES!

*OR, KING HENRY VIII. AND THE ABBOT OF
READING.*

~~~~~~~~~~~~~~~~~~~~~~~~

A LITTLE boy stood gazing at a pastrycook's fair
    tray,
Where tarts, and puffs, and lollipops were spread in
    sweet array.
He stood and gazed, but that was all, he could not
    purchase any,
Because, like Simple Simon, he hadn't got a penny ;
When by there came an uncle, of broad and portly
    trim,
And he looked down at his nephew, and his nephew
    looked at him.
" My dearest boy," the uncle said, in solemn tone and
    gruff,
"You really don't think you could eat all that un-
    wholesome stuff ? "

"Oh, uncle dear," in tones of cheer, that nephew
    made reply,

"I don't quite know what I could do, but I *should*
    like to try."

"Alas, alas!" the uncle said, and rather sighed than
    smiled,

"I would I were again a boy, an artless, happy
    child!

What pure and simple pleasure from that stall I then
    might buy,

But now I couldn't touch a tart, and I shouldn't
    like to try."

The nephew stood expectant; the uncle did not
    mind;

So the boy said, "Sir, in 'Fuller' a prescription you
    will find."

The uncle turned him homewards with a slow and
    heavy tread,

Then o'er a ponderous volume before him open
    spread,

He sat and pored for many hours; he did not go to
    bed;

And this, or something like it, was the story which he
    read.

"Merry it is in the good greenwood,
    When the mavis and merle are singing,

When the deer sweeps by, and the hounds are in
 cry,
 And the hunter's horn is ringing."
Thus cries Sir Walter, in heart-stirring song,
  And I think you will say,
  In a general way,
That the Bard of the North is "no that far wrong."

  But 'tis not quite so merry,
  Indeed it is very
Provoking and trying, to saint or to sinner,
  When you find, to your cost,
  That your way you have lost,
And that dinner-time's come, and brought with it no
 dinner;
While your friends are so far that nought 'twill avail ye
To sound the wild *mort* or the jolly *reveillé!*

  For James Fitz-James
  The poet claims
That he didn't get cross and call his knights
 "names;"
  And though it is clear
  He had some cause for fear,
And the loss of his steed made him feel rather queer,
He said nothing worse than—"Beshrew yon wild
 deer."

But King Hal the Bluff
Was of different stuff,
And his language and manners were both somewhat
    rough,
So he fretted and fumed far more than enough,
Vowed his grand M. F. H. was " a regular muff,"
And declared that not one of his dastardly train
Should ever go hunting with him again !

Nor cooled was the fire
Of the monarch's ire ;
In fact, it flamed up considerably higher,
When—his exit made
From the forest glade
And the sylvan shade
Formed by lofty trees with their branches spreading,
He found that his ride
Had been towards the wrong side,
And instead of to Windsor had brought him to
   Reading !

He was burly and tall,
But he felt quite small,
As he thought how that moment in Windsor Hall,
The banquet was led by the seneschal,
And the vassals were feasting, one and all,
While their lord and master was far beyond call.

The thought was as bitter as wormwood and
    gall !
And he wrathfully muttered, " I call it a *shame;* "
Though he knew he had only himself to blame.
For that morn he had tenderly said to his Kate,
" If I'm not home to dinner, love, pray do not
    wait."
        Stay, though, I can't state
        Precisely the date
Of my story, and so I'm unable to fix
        Which queen then did reign ;
        If not Kate, 'tis plain
        'Twas Anne, or else Jane,
For their names were but three, though their number
    was six.

        Oh, free and fair is Reading town !
        And rich and rare is her high renown
For biscuits, baked of a nice light brown !
        Mixed, milk, and Marie,
        Rural, rusk, ratafia,
        Toast, table, and tea,
        Orange, Osborne, Oswego, and mild nursery,
With many more names, I'll not stop to rehearse,
For colonials and captains won't fit in my verse ;
Yet I think you'll agree that King Hal had been
    calmer

If in his knapsack
He'd the forethought to pack
Some few dozens of these—made by Huntley and
    Palmer.

But Palmers then
Were a sort of men
Who wore cockle-shells and sandal shoon :
    Carried staves and scrips,
    Fed on haws and hips,
And shrank e'en from touching a macaroon.
Quoth the King, with a sigh, as one rudely awaked,
"Don't count on your biscuits before they are baked."

But stay, oh stay !
That abbey grey,
On Forbery Hill, not far away,
Was built, so at least all the guide-books say,
By King Henry the First (surnamed *Beauclerc)*
As a penance for injuries done to his *Frère*
Duke Robert, King William's lawful heir.
    Henry did not choose
    To wear peas in his shoes,
Or to walk barefoot among brambles and briars,
    So this abbey he built
    To atone for his guilt,
And left to the rule of the Benedict Friars.

The stately pile was his glory and pride
While he lived, and they buried him there when he
    died.
King Henry the Eighth, now relieved from anxiety,
Felt inclined to approve of his ancestor's piety.

Full sweet is the sound of the convent bell
As it ringeth clearly o'er wood and dell,
For it speaketh of peace, and of calm repose,
Of respite alike from friends and from foes,
From courtly pageants and empty shows,
From morning calls and similar woes,
From little girls wanting new Sunday clothes,
And boys with their boots always out at the toes !
       On the monarch's ear
       Most sweet and clear,
With sound of hope and presage of cheer,
       Fell the solemn swell
       Of that abbey bell.
For it rang not for matins, nor yet for compline,
But it said very plainly, " Oh, come, come and dine."
And the King, spurring fast towards Forbery Hill,
Replied with great fervour, " Ay, marry, I will."

Now Bluff King Hal was fond of a joke,
So he took off his crown, popped it into his " poke,"
And, disguising himself, merely sent in his card

As a "Yeoman, one of his Majesty's Guard,"
And was quickly seated among the rest,
The Lord Abbot's own particular guest.
"For, good friend," thus remarked his lordship's grace,
"Thou bearest thy passport in figure and face;
'Twas ever thus, since his reign began,
Our royal master loveth a *man.*"

　　　Good St. Benedict
　　　Was uncommonly strict,
And drew up his rules with the utmost decorum
(The monks often thought, on purpose to bore 'em)
In Latin, the *Regula Monachorum.*
　　　" Poor fellow, you know,
　　　He lived long ago ! "
Quoth the Abbot, "for our times his notions are
　　　' slow.'
To adhere to these rules means simply starvation,
And I think 'tis allowed to one of my station
To give to the Latin a free translation ! "

　　　So the King soon found
　　　On looking around,
He'd no need to complain of the monkish board ;
　　　For the table was filled,
　　　Thus the Abbot willed,
With all dainties the farm or the field could afford.

There was chicken and ham,
And mint sauce and lamb,
Good things which no cook should e'er part in
sunder, but
What pleased the King most
Was the knightly roast,
A sirloin of beef, with a very prime undercut.
To make its acquaintance he was full fain,
'Twas cut, and come, and come again !

The monks all gazed
At their guest amazed,
As his knife and fork played a yeoman's part ;
And when finished at last
Was the brave repast,
The Abbot exclaimed : " Well fare thy heart !
Come, pledge me now this cup of sack
To thy master's health.   May he never lack
Such men as thou to eat and to fight !
If our properest men must needs be our chief eaters,
The royal warrant was surely right
Which named thee one of his Majesty's Beef-eaters !
An hundred pounds would I gladly pay
Could *I* make such a meal as thou this day !

But alas, with me,
Few things will agree,

To touch solid meat is rarely my habit;
       I scarce can digest
       A slice from the breast
Of a tender chicken, or little young rabbit!"
The King sympathised, tried to look tender-hearted,
Thanked his host for good cheer, and so departed.

       Some weeks passed away,
       Then, one sorrowful day
       To that abbey grey
Came a messenger nobody dared disobey;
A Royal Pursuivant, with warrant of power
To take the Lord Abbot at once to the Tower.

       When there he was fed
       Upon water and bread;
He bewailed his hard fate; many tears he shed,
He really did not feel sure that his head
Was safe on his shoulders, so great was his dread;
And he spent all his time in trying to measure
The how and the why of the King's displeasure.
Yet he felt a sensation of joy and relief,
A welcome diversion from sorrow and grief,
       When the warder at last,
       To end his long fast,
Brought in a magnificent sirloin of beef.

Then forgetting all fears of bodily harm,
He ate like a farmer just fresh from the farm,
No longer he shrank from beef or from mutton :
" Two hungry meals make the third a glutton."

King Hal, from a private lobby hard by,
On his lordship's actions had played the spy ;
And now springing in, he exclaimed with glee,
" How now, my Lord Abbot, right gladly I see
That my patient is cured, so pay me my fee !
An hundred pounds of good red gold
Must upon this table be duly told,
Or the monks of Reading may wait in vain
To welcome their Lord Abbot home again."

The Abbot, full glad to be quit of his fright,
Obeyed with as good a grace as he might ;
Then reached down his crozier, and put on his mitre,
And went home with a heart and a purse somewhat
    lighter.

       *   *   *   *   *   *

The morning dawns, the uncle yawns, and shuts the
    weighty book,
Then hies him to the fair abode of the tempting
    pastrycook ;

He purchases the stock-in-trade of cakes, and tarts,
    and pies,
Then finds his gentle nephew, and unto him he cries,
" My dearest boy, eat all you can, and give the rest
    away
Unto your youthful playfellows, so happy and so gay,
But oh, I pray, be moderate, or plainly I foresee,
'Tis you will need the doctor, and who then will pay
    the fee ? "
Three ringing cheers the uncle hears, then turns him
    to depart,
Yet beareth homeward for his share a large red-
    currant tart !

COUNT RUDOLPH'S BEARD.

A TALE OF CHIVALRY.

COUNT RUDOLPH VON RATZ was a noble knight,
Quite ready at all times to dance or to fight;
His name was a terror to every foe,
His battle-axe dealt a most deadly blow;
He usually fought with a dozen or so
At once, but that was the custom, you know,
In the knightly days of long ago,
When to fight with one man was accounted "low,"
For a noble knight not at all *comme il faut !*
While in softer mood, all the world would agree,
None bowed with more courtly grace than he,
Or more featly served, on his bended knee,
The ladies at tennis or afternoon tea.
In short, he was equally loved and feared ;
And besides,—he possessed such a *gem* of a beard !
      'Twas soft, and long,
        And silky, and brown ;
The boast of the country, the talk of the town ;

The envy of many a beardless youth
Who dashed down razor, and groaned, forsooth,
    In wan despair !
    For the unguents rare
Of Rowland, Latreille, or Professor Brown
    Could never produce
    E'en by constant use
Such a beard as grew, quite spontaneously,
On the chin of Count Rudolph, surnamed the Free !

And many a maid heaved a secret sigh
As the knight on his coal-black steed rode by ;
And delicate fingers would often trace
On banner of silk, or cigarette case,
The arms that flashed on his silver shield,
The arms that none but he might wield :
Two hairy oobits proper upon a verdant field !

    But little recked he,
    This knight so free,
Of youth who frowned, or of maid who sighed ;
And he laughed out loud as he gaily cried,
" Come weal, or come woe, the whole of my trade is
To fight all the knights, and to serve all the ladies ;
Yet nor knight nor maiden of high degree
Shall e'er boast of the capture of Rudolph the Free."

Full oft the pitcher may go to the well,
Yet one day ringeth its funeral knell !
       And " the god of love
       Who sits above "
(So Shakespeare says, and he's always right)
Sent a shaft to the heart of the careless knight,
       Who turned round quick
       And, like Benedick,
Thus all tiresome jokes on the subject parried :
       " When I vowed that I
       Would a bachelor die,
I did not think I should live to be married ! "

On a " castled crag " by the " lonely Rhine "
Dwelt the lordly Baron von Blumenstein ;
       And henchmen true
       In doublets of blue,
Who mostly had nothing at all to do,
Stood waiting about, in doorway and hall,
In case the Baron should please to call,
" What ho, without there ! " (in tone of dread),
" Remove the banquet," or " somebody's head."
'Twas all the same to those vassals bold,
Who did, without murmur, just what they were told ;
Or I trow there'd have been what is termed " a
    shine "
In the stately halls of Blumenstein !

The Baron was blessed with a gentle wife,
The joy of his heart and the pride of his life ;
She never spoke word that engendered strife ;
     But cabbages red
     She pickled instead,
She rose with the lark, and went early to bed.
The fame of her beer and *sauer-kraut*
Was noised through the country round about :
And the Baron's retainers would often vow
That no lord in the land had a better *Haus-frau.*

     But beyond compare
     Was the daughter fair
Who graced the home of the worthy pair.
She had lovely blue eyes and bright golden hair,
And plenty of frocks all of white to wear ;
She'd a heart quite light and free from care,
And cheeks like the blush on the Cath'rine pear ;
Such a winsome smile, such a charming air
Would have softened the heart of a grizzly bear ;
And before you had time to say " Beware ! "
Every youth who beheld her began to pine
For the love of sweet Hilda von Blumenstein.
     I trow, there is little need for me
     To tell any lover of chivalry
That this was the lady of high degree
Who was born to lead captive Rudolph the Free.

Behold him now, as he kneels at her feet,
And pleadeth his cause in accents sweet :
" Let my love be proven, my lady fair,
Show me what for thy sake I shall do or dare,
And 'tis done at once, whatever it be,
For thou alone rulest o'er Rudolph the Free."

The lady blushed, and the lady sighed ;
She knew that his love would be sorely tried.
" Now lithe and listen, sir knight," quoth she,
" I claim no service of bended knee,
I put thy love to no simple test
Of doughty deed or of knightly quest ;
Far harder task must, I ween, be thine
Ere thou winnest Hilda von Blumenstein."

" Now prove me, and try me, my lady fair,
What man may do, or what man may dare,
That Rudolph dares, for thy sake, to try ;
An he fail or falter, then let him die."

Full sweetly smiled that lady bright,
To hear the vow of her gallant knight ;
Yet ashen pale grew her lovely cheek,
And vainly awhile she strove to speak ;
But at last came the words which to breathe she
  feared,
The tremulous murmur, " Cut off thy beard ! "

With sudden anger the knight flushed red,
" Nay, lady mine," he proudly said,
" Hadst thou asked for my heart, or my hand, or my
       head,
The thing were more quickly done than said ;
But I trow 'tis merely a mockery
To lay such command on Rudolph the Free."

"Alack and alas," the lady cried,
" My love for thee overcometh my pride ;
Yet never mayst thou be knight of mine,
For thus runs the legend of Blumenstein :

" ' 𝔚𝔥𝔢𝔫 a 𝔩𝔞𝔡𝔶 𝔬𝔣 𝔅𝔩𝔲𝔪𝔢𝔫𝔰𝔱𝔢𝔦𝔫, 𝔣𝔞𝔦𝔯 𝔞𝔫𝔡 𝔟𝔯𝔦𝔤𝔥𝔱,
𝔖𝔥𝔞𝔩𝔩 𝔩𝔦𝔰𝔱 𝔱𝔬 𝔱𝔥𝔢 𝔩𝔬𝔟𝔢 𝔬𝔣 𝔞 𝔟𝔢𝔞𝔯𝔡𝔢𝔡 𝔨𝔫𝔦𝔤𝔥𝔱,
𝔄 𝔠𝔯𝔶 𝔰𝔥𝔞𝔩𝔩 𝔟𝔢 𝔥𝔢𝔞𝔯𝔡 𝔞𝔱 𝔡𝔢𝔞𝔡 𝔬𝔣 𝔫𝔦𝔤𝔥𝔱,
𝔄𝔫𝔡 𝔣𝔦𝔯𝔢 𝔞𝔫𝔡 𝔣𝔩𝔞𝔪𝔢 𝔯𝔬𝔲𝔰𝔢 𝔱𝔥𝔢 𝔴𝔞𝔯𝔡𝔢𝔯𝔰 𝔞𝔩𝔩
𝔗𝔥𝔞𝔱 𝔨𝔢𝔢𝔭 𝔱𝔥𝔢𝔦𝔯 𝔴𝔞𝔱𝔠𝔥 𝔬𝔫 𝔱𝔥𝔢 𝔠𝔞𝔰𝔱𝔩𝔢 𝔴𝔞𝔩𝔩 ! '

"Our castle is planned by my lordly sire,
Who feareth no foe save the crafty fire !
In every bower is a hand-grenade ;
In the courtyard, a volunteer fire-brigade ;
O'er each noble steed, as he standeth in stall,
Hangs the harness ready at need to fall ;
In every corridor, I ween,
Gleams the scarlet robe of the fire-queen,

With her motto which speaketh to every one :
'Place thine arms through the straps and run.'
Yet, I fear me that all would naught avail,
Should Hilda list to thy flatt'ring tale."

"Now Fate divides us," Sir Rudolph said,
" Were ever lovers so sore bested ?
For a withered crone o'er my cradle sung
This ancient rhyme in an ancient tongue :

" ' 𝔚𝔦𝔱𝔥 𝔥𝔢𝔞𝔩𝔱𝔥 𝔞𝔫𝔡 𝔴𝔦𝔱𝔥 𝔰𝔱𝔯𝔢𝔫𝔤𝔱𝔥 𝔱𝔥𝔶 𝔟𝔢𝔞𝔯𝔡 𝔰𝔥𝔞𝔩𝔩 𝔤𝔯𝔬𝔴,
    𝔍𝔫 𝔣𝔦𝔯𝔢 𝔞𝔫𝔡 𝔣𝔩𝔞𝔪𝔢 '𝔱𝔴𝔦𝔩𝔩 𝔳𝔞𝔫𝔦𝔰𝔥, 𝔍 𝔱𝔯𝔬𝔴.'

"Yet say but the word, and e'en Fate I brave,
For Rudolph the Free is thine humble slave."

      "Nay now, nay now,
      'Twere vain, I trow,
To Fate's decree to refuse to bow ;
      An thou diedst," quoth she,
      " All for love of me,
I don't think matters improved would be—
So I think, on the whole, I'll go home to tea.
And I charge thee for ever all hope to resign
Of wedding Hilda von Blumenstein."

      By the castle gate,
      When night fell late,
Linger'd Rudolph von Ratz, in a doleful state ;

On a Hebrew harp he sadly played,
And he sang to his lady a serenade ;—
His words and his tune ne'er had met before,
And 'twere much to be wished they should meet no
 more ;
'Tis ill to sing when the heart is sore.

On the ear of the watchful sentinel
The sound discordant at midnight fell,
And he said to himself : " This is not well."
So, raising his crossbow high in the air,
He sternly demanded, " Who goes there ? "
  But the knight, I suppose,
  Was lost in his woes,
And he only longed to disturb the repose
Of the maiden who caused to his heart such
 throes ;
So he went on chanting his tuneless prayer,
" Awake and listen, O lady fair ! "

  I pause to remark
  That the night it was dark ;
And the sentinel, fearing to make a mistake,
Came up to the knight, gave his shoulder a shake,
As a gentle hint for the worst to prepare,
And repeated his query of " Who goes there ? "
But Rudolph still called on his lady fair.

The watchman, his patience exhausted quite,
Determined to view the stranger aright,
Put his hand in his pocket, to feel for a light,
Struck a match on the box (it was Bryant and
    May's),
And the beard of the knight was soon in a blaze!

A cry of " fire " through the still night rang,
Loud pealed the alarm-bell with crash and with
    clang ;
And out came pouring the warders all,
Who kept their watch on the castle wall.
In fifty seconds, or rather less,
The engine came dashing along express ;
Quick the firemen saw where the mischief lay,
So they " married their stand-pipes " without delay,
And straight on Count Rudolph began to play,
While the trusty henchmen formed in a line
And passed the buckets right up from the Rhine ;
And the Baron himself, his wife, and his daughter,
Descended by rope-ladders into the water.

     'Twas a terrible rout,
     Though the fire was put out
Ere Rudolph quite knew what 'twas all about ;
     But alas and alack !
     A remnant black

Alone remained, for the world to see,
Of the noble beard of Count Rudolph the Free.
A passing sigh for that vanished grace,
Count Rudolph heaved for a moment's space ;
'Twas a thousand pities he wasn't insured,
But he thought, " 'Tis an evil that cannot be cured,
So I trow it will e'en have to be endured."
Then a sudden joy through his bosom thrilled !
" Beshrew me, the portents are both fulfilled !
And no one's the worse, except by a fright,
Sir Rudolph, no longer a bearded knight—
May claim the hand of his lady bright ! "
So he did.   And the bells rang right merrily
For the wedding of Hilda with Rudolph the Free.

BRIMMACUM'S UMBRELLA.

BRIMMACUM'S our second master—he's rather a mild
    sort of " fella,"
But at Easter-time he went and bought the gor-
    geous*est* umbrella !
There's too many syllables there for the grammar, I
    must confess ;
But anything falling short of those words my feel-
    ings wouldn't express !
'Twas silk, with an ebony stick, and gold mounts, or
    something as bright,
And topped up with a jolly big ball of the finest
    crocidolite—
That's right, I know, for I bribed little Jones with my
    penknife (I wanted to sell it),
To go up to Brimmacum's desk one day, and ask
    him how to spell it !
My ! wasn't he mad ? But he'd have been worse if
    he'd heard Briggs major reporting,
" I say, boys, here's a precious lark ; old Brim-
    macum's going a-courting."

3

Well, the summer holidays came and went—we
    always come back a bit glum ;
But worse than the newest homesick boy was poor
    old Brimmacum.
That the course of true love hadn't run smooth, was
    plain to the seeing eye,
For his smart umbrella had disappeared, and none
    knew the reason why.
And Briggs *did* say—but Briggs, I fear, for truth
    doesn't greatly care—
That he'd changed it away for a diamond ring, which
    the lady declined to wear.

I didn't go home at Christmas time ; I went up
    north to see
The splendidest man that ever lived—my grand-
    father, Squire Leigh.
And didn't I have a glorious time, a regular first-
    rate spree !
        There was skating and riding,
        Snowballing and sliding,
    And everything fine in the way of providing ;
        Turkeys and geese,
        Ten mince-pies apiece,
    And carol singers unmoved by police ;
        Holly and yew,
        And snapdragon, too,
    With a big plum-pudding, all burning blue !

Hunt the slipper and blind-man's buff,
Figs and oranges *quantum suff.*
(A piece of Latin no boy finds tough).
Roast apples and chestnuts, all aglow ;
Playing upon the old banjo—
I mean the boys, not the apples, you
know—
Doing our best to " jump Jim Crow,"
Kissing under the mistletoe
(But that's a proceeding I think rather slow),
Getting back forfeits lost at " old sodger,"
And then—Aunt Lucy struck up " Sir Roger."

Aunt Lucy's capital fun when nobody else is by ;
She likes a lark as well as a boy, if it's only done on
the sly ;
But when there are other fellows about—big grown-
up fellows I mean—
She puts on all her fine lady airs, and remembers
she's turned eighteen ;
And instead of waiting upon a chap, and putting his
specimens right,
She expects him to dangle after her, and be what
she calls " polite ! "
So when the dancing and stuff began, I wasn't going
to stay ;
I saw Aunt Lucy looking for me, and I quietly
slipped away.

I went to call on the keeper—his name is old Joe
    Tupper ;
I thought I'd have a good talk with him, and get
    back in time for supper.

I love to talk to old keeper Joe, because he can
    always tell a
Good tale about hunting or fishing, or, what I like
    almost as well, a
        Ghost story that might
        Make your hair stand upright,
And give you the "creeps" for the rest of the
        night ;
        A terrible tale of a woman in white,
        With golden hair and eyes as bright
        As the newest thing in electric light,
Which wildly gleam o'er flood and fell—a
        Story of fear
        For the time of year ;
But the only thing I did not think to hear
Was the story of—Brimmacum's best umbrella.

        There it stood on the cottage floor,
        The very first thing my eyes before,
        When, stealing away from that wild uproar,
        I gently opened the keeper's door !
        It looked at me with an eye severe ;
        I fell back, muttering, " This is queer."

But, growing bolder, I ventured near,
Saying, " How in the world did you get
here ? "

Then keeper Joe, rising, cheerily said,
" I'm main glad to see thee, Maister Fred.
Cum, sit thee down, and I'll tell thee t' story
O' that there umbrella what's stannin' afore
thee."
I obeyed his behest right cheerfully,
And I'll tell you the tale as 'twas told to me.

" Miss Lucy, thou knows, she cum back fra school
chock full o' all sorts o' knowledge ;
But all th' lot on't wurn't no use—she wanted to go
to t' college.
The lasses i' my young days, Maister Fred, they
hadn't so far to seek ;
They'd nobbut one tongue, and they used it—they
wanted no Latin nor Greek ;
They looked arter housekeepin' matters, they baked
t' puddin's and t' pies,
And if ivver their tongues did fail 'em, why, they
made it up with their eyes.
But t' squire got a schoolmaister fella to cum i' th'
holiday time,
And he wur a-teachin' Miss Lucy thro' all th'
summer's prime.

Aye, but Miss Lucy's a scholard, and she went at it
　　right smart ;
And it tuk her just no time at all to get all his books
　　by heart.
'Twould ha' done ye good to hear 'em talk o' the
　　glorious ' Tragic Three ' ;
But th' thing as puzzled me most o' all were th'
　　wondrous ' Attic Bee.'
Thinks I,—' I beant no scholard, and he's got th'
　　mathematics ;
But I don't believe as his bees 'ud thrive, if he kep'
　　'em up i' the attics ! '
Yet howsomedivver that might be, there wurn't no
　　lack o' honey,
And their books was allus a-preachin' up the wuth-
　　lessness of money,
　For money can't gi'e happiness '—thinks I, ' That's
　　pretty plain ;
Umbrellas don't bring t'sunshine, but they helps
　　to keep out t' rain.'
Then he tuk her out i' the park o' nights, and he larnt
　　her t' names o' t' stars,
And he tauld her which wur Venus, and which wur
　　Cupid and Mars ;
And they went a-streakin' about i' th' lanes in a
　　manner most surprisin',
And they brought home a heap of rubbishly weeds,
　　and said they wur botanizin'.

They calls him Miss Lucy's "coach,"' says I,
  ' missus, but dosta know?
If they'd on'y gi'en him to me to name, I'd ha' called
  him Miss Lucy's beau.'
And so fur a week or two, thou knows, he had it all
  his own way ;
But then t' auld house begun to fill wi' folks as had
  cum to stay.
Miss Lucy kep' up wi' her lessons, as in course she
  wur bound to do,
But he fun hissen at loose ends like, arter they'd
  gotten thro' ;
For he wurn't at home a-top on a horse, and wur
  mortal feared on a gun ;
And Miss Lucy went off wi' her cousins, and he wur
  clean out o' t' fun.
So he turned quite sulky-like, and cum off a-fishin',
  ye see,
And he thought he'd show off his larnin', and hev it
  out wi' me ;
But, bless ye, I knows a sight o' things, so I wurn't
  taken aback,
For Trigonometry beant no use when ye're gettin' a
  barn to thack ;
And I onct heard Miss Lucy say to him—she knowed
  she wur talkin' treason,
' You men invented logic fur to hide your want o'
  reason.'

Well, he sets hissen down alongside o' me, and maks
    believe to fish,
(Ye might put all the trout as he ivver caught in a
    very small-sized dish).
Then all on a sudden he bursts out, wi'out the least
    apology :
        Says he, ' Joe,
        Dosta know
Aught about Chro-nology ? '
        Says I, ' Nay,
        I can't rightly say,
As I ivver did much i' that sort o' way.'
' Aye, that's a terrible pity,' says he ;
' It's a very gran' science, Chro-nol-o-gy.
It taks in all creeturs, great and small,
The fishes that swim and the beasties that crawl,
And shows ye some things as ye can't see at all ;

" ' It classifies ants, and blue-bottle flies,
And teaches ye how to make use on your eyes.'
Thinks I to mysen, ' Ah, thou may boast,
I can see as far thro' a mileston' as most,
Tho' I ne'er i' my life set foot in a college.'   He
        Goes on, wi' a laugh,
         ' 'Twould take thee half
O' the rest o' thy life to larn Chronology ;
But I'll lend thee a hand, if to larn 't thou'rt
    wishin'.'

'Thou don't say so,' says I ;
'Well, I think I'll none try,
So I'll e'en get along wi' my fishin'.'

" Just then I landed a fine fat trout,
And t' schoolmaister thought as I'd cut him out ;
So, as soon as t' fish wur fairly caught,
' Joe,' he begins,' ' dosta know aught
        O' t' science o' Phrenolo-gy ? '
        Says I to he,
        ' What might that be ?
I doubt 'twould be summat too strong for me.'
' Oh, that,' says he, ' rings i' th' student's ears
Th' wonderful music of the spheres ;
And numbers the countless orbs that stray
Thro' the trackless path o' the Milky Way ;
It shows how the planets in order run ;
It weighs the earth, and it measures the sun,
With a science exact, that never fails.'
Thinks I, ' But I'd like to look at them scales ! '

    " ' It's a gran' thing, ye see,
        Is Phrenolo-gy.
'Twould tak half thy lifetime to larn 't,' says he.
Says I, ' I'm afeard it's no good wishin',
        Fur as yet I ne'er
        Had that time to spare,
So I'll e'en get along wi' my fishin'.'

" Then he drops his rod, of its weight com-
    plainin',
Puts up his umbrella, and thinks it's rainin',
    Wonders why he cum,
    Thinks he'll go home,
Then all on a sudden, ' Joe,' he cries,
    ' Open thy eyes,
That flower o' the rock's a splendid prize !
    I mun get it fur her ; '—
    I didn't stir,
It wurn't no manner o' use to me.
' Why, Joe,' a'most in a passion, cries he,
' Thou cannot know Ornitholo-gy ;
That tells ye the name o' each flower as blows,
From the daisy pied to the blushing rose ;
It puts each plant o' thy cottage border
Into its proper system and order ;
And by its help ye can easily settle
Which part is the stamen and which is the petal.
Aye, sad indeed must thy lack o' knowledge be !
'Twould tak' half thy life to larn Ornithology ! '
Says I, ' Fur larnin' I'm allus a-wishin',
    When I've naught else to do ;
    But I think that noo
'Twould be best fur me t' get on wi' my fishin' ! !

" Then he gangs a-slitherin' about them rocks ;
But t' flower all his tewin' and moilin' mocks,

And afore I 'xactly sees what he's arter,
He pitches head-foremost into t' water!
But, as luck would hev' it, that smart umbrella
(A long sight too smart fur a schoolmaister fella)
Sticks fast i' t' rocks, so he holds on tight,
And he hollers fur me wi' all his might.
Thinks I, ' Thy larnin's a poor apology.'
    ' Schoolmaister,' says I,
      ' Didst ivver try
To larn t' science o' *Swimology?* '
      Says he, ' No ;
      Mak' haste, Joe ;
      If you don't be quick I shall *hev'* to let go.'
Says I, as I plunged i' th' stream like winkin',
And landed him drippin' upon the shore,
' If I hadn't lookt sharp 'twou'd ha' tuk thee
    more
Nor the WHOLE O' THY LIFE to larn that, I'm
    thinkin' ! '

" Yet he wur a plucky chap, arter all, fur he cum back
    t' next day,
And pulled that flower fur Miss Lucy, but I think she
    said him nay ;
Leastwise, he seemed down-hearted like, when he
    cum to say good-bye ;
But mebbe he couldn't mak' up his mind, and so wur
    afeard to try.

He wanted to gi'e me a fi'-pun note, and that's how
  it cum to pass
As he left me his smart umbrella, fur I wouldn't ha'
  none on his brass.
So I've got it fur a keepsake, fur I really tuk it kind
On him to be so anxious fur t' improvin' o' my
  mind ! "

I told Aunt Lucy the story, but she didn't see the
  fun,
Though I left out all the lovering, as, of course, Joe
  should have done.
And though I didn't mention names—a fact I can
  aver,
She *cried* because old Brimmacum had risked his life
  for her !
Well, girls are the queerest creatures, that's all I've
  got to say ;
And I think (but you mustn't let it out, or hint it in
  any way,
'Tis a secret I've never told before, not e'en to my
  nearest chum)
That very soon I shall have to speak—of—" My
  Uncle Brimmacum."
I think 'twill be rather jolly, you know, for he isn't
  half a bad " fella,"
And my wedding present to him shall be another
  fine umbrella !

BRIMMACUM'S WEDDING.

WHEN Christmas-time came round again, and flung
    o'er hill and lake
A veil of snow, like frosting on a jolly rich plum-
    cake ;
And Winter, like a pastrycook, the ice was deftly
    spreading,
Aunt Lucy sent me a silver card to bid me to Brim-
    macum's wedding.
There were two little hearts in the corner, instead of
    a postage-stamp ;
And Hymen larking round with his torch, which
    looked like a bicycle lamp ;
And ivy (that means Fidelity) with true-lovers' knots
    in a bow :
When I make up *my* mind to get married, I won't be
    so spoony, I know.

Aunt Lucy wrote, "Dearest Freddie" (*Freddie!* I
    was in a rage),
" I thought you might like to come, dear, and be my
    sweet little page ! "—

Now I don't care much for pages, they're mostly
    dressed-up girls,
With lace furbelows and collars and a lot of un-
    cropped curls,
And they hang about with the horses, instead of
    going to fight ;
So I thought, all things considered, I'd rather be a
    knight.
Briggs major chaffed me awfully ; said he, " It's jolly
    grand
To be Brimmacum's boy in buttons," which of course
    I couldn't stand.

So we two concocted a pretty note, which said I'd
    gladly come
And shed the light of my presence on Mrs. Brim-
    macum ;
But if 'twas all the same to her, for reasons I'd not
    explain,
I'd rather be H. M. Stanley, or Allan Quatermain ;—
Or, if she went for the classics, as far as I could tell,
Why, Ajax or Dick Turpin would suit me just as
    well !

But my brilliant suggestions experienced a rebuff,
For she thought the last-named gentlemen a little
    bit too rough,
And of juvenile explorers she'd really had enough ;

I didn't think Aunt Lucy remembered things so
    long,—
To rake up a fellow's sins like that, is downright
    mean and wrong.
She was hinting at that afternoon we started for the
    Cape,
Got shipwrecked in the greenhouse, and cleared off
    every grape.
Old Joe said, "Boys is varmint "—but I forgave him
    then ;
I know he's not the sort of chap to bring things up
    again.

So, after all, it was settled I'd better be myself.
And then (at the end of the term, you know, one's
    apt to be short of pelf,
But the *mater* came down handsome, she thought it
    very nice)
I bought a fine umbrella, and I stuffed it full of
    rice ;
And I made old Brimmacum promise, whatever was
    the weather,
He wouldn't put it up until his bride and he were
    together !
It *was* the tallest kind of a joke, because, you see, it
    appears
They'd agreed to pretend they'd been married for
    any amount of years ;

And nobody had the least notion they were out on
    their honeymoon
(Folks must have been precious stupid, for I lay they
    did nothing but spoon).
But, one day, when lots of swells were round, it came
    on to rain,—in a trice
Up went that smart umbrella, and out fell a ·shower
    of rice !
Oh ! didn't the people chaff them, and there was no
    end of a spree !
And the credit of that transaction was entirely due to *me*.

But there, as the bookwriting fellows say, " we must
    not anticipate."
I reached Leigh Hall " the day before," which I
    thought was rather late ;
Still, I had my share in the scrimmage, for, after a
    minute's doubt,
Grandmother said that Ethel and I might set the
    presents out—
Ethel's the youngest bridesmaid ; we had a bit of a
    wrangle,
She called old Brimmacum " a duck," because he
    gave her a bangle ;
And she was uncommonly wild with me, though it
    wasn't the slightest use,
When I said I didn't know much about ducks, but I
    fancied she was a goose !

Well, we made it up in a little while,
Then settled to work in first-rate style ;
We wrote some neat little labels, and counted them
up when we'd done ;
And the glorious sum total—was three hundred and
sixty-one !
Presents aren't half a bad invention—
Just a few I should like to mention :
A patent contrivance for drawing a cork,
Three dozen spoons and a toasting-fork ;
Knives for carving and eating fishes,
And fifteen designs in butter-dishes ;
A silver "grid " for frying your steak,
And little twin baskets for wedding-cake ;
A set of sermons from Uncle Draper
(He'd better have sent the "Boy's Own
Paper ") ;
Bowls and plates, and such like crocks,
Garden-rollers, and chiming clocks ;
The stunningest sort of a writing-table,
Six pen-wipers from baby Mabel ;
Scuttles for coals, and silver lamps,
And the Wonderland Case for postage-stamps ;
Brooches and bracelets set with jewels,
And heaps and heaps of things in crewels,
Which Ethel tremendously admired,
Though the very sight of them made me tired.

4

Up to this, we'd behaved with the greatest pro-
    priety,
But now I proposed that, by way of variety,
A little amusement might intervene,
So I popped the pug in the soup-tureen,
And suggested the wall-pocket lined with satin
Was exactly the place to hide the cat in !
I'd just accomplished my dearest wish
By putting a mouse in the muffin-dish,
When the ink-stand went and toppled over,
So I stopped the stream with a table-cover ;
But Ethel cried out, "Oh dear, oh dear !
That's the gift of the Lady Delamere ! "
'Twas plain I'd got into an awful mess,
So I thought I'd better go and confess ;
But, though perhaps 'twas a trifle mean,
I couldn't help feeling more serene
When Granny came peering round the screen.
She gazed awhile on that Stygian scene,
And then only said, very soft and low,
She thought, on the whole, I had better go
And pay a visit to keeper Joe
(Just to keep me out of a scrape, you know),
While she and Ethel set matters straight.
That cleared my mind of a heavy weight
And I feel at liberty to state
That the damage wasn't so very great.

As I drew near to the cottage-door, Old Brimmacum
    walked away ;
Cried Joe, " I'm fain to see thee, lad, and hopes thou
    bee'st cum to stay !
Says I to th' missis, ' He's sewer to cum, or else thou
    may ca' me dunce.'
Schule-maister's bin argufyin' wi' me as a man can't
    luv but once ;
Says I, wi' my face pulled straight-like, tho' I
    laughed a bit i' my sleeve,
' Maister, an true luv cums but onc't, there's a sight
    o' mak'-believe ! '
But theer, what can ye 'spect of a chap o' th' eve on
    his weddin'-day ?
When folk is bent on coortin', they're apt to be tuk
    i' that way."

       Here I broke in with, " Joe, I say,
       You've led me astray,
       You told me Aunt Lucy had said him ' nay ! ' "
       Joe answered me in his solemn way,
";Maister Fred, an thou lives long eneugh, it's sartin
    thou wilt find
A woman's none a woman, if she doesn't chaange
    her mind !
That minds me on a story as chanced i' my young days;
Cum, sit thee down and hear it; I'll mak' t' fire t' blaze.

"Sally and Sam, when I wur young, had coorted
　　mony a year,
And a' th' folk they wished 'em well as knowed 'em,
　　far and near.
An' they wur happy, I'll be boun', as any lark as
　　sings ;
For Sally wur a gradely lass, as knowed the mak' o'
　　things,
An' Sam nor all th' other lads wur taller by th' head ;
An' 'twas th' talk o' t' village as they wur boun' to
　　wed.
Now, on a summer's evenin', when t' farm-work wur
　　all done,
They walked togither, arm-in-arm, and Sam he thus
　　begun :
　　　　　'Sally,' says he,
　　　　　' Thee an' me
　　　'S been a coortin' a goodish bit, hanna we ? '
　　　Sally blushed and smiled and looked away ;
　　　She thought, in course he wur goin' to say,
　　　' My lass, now I wants thee to name t' day.'
　　　And so she wur summat taken aback,
　　　When he went on quite anither tack.
' Hey, we've been a coortin' a longish bit—but 'tis
　　over'd now, I find ;
So I thought I'd cum an' tell thee as I ha' chaanged
　　my mind.'

" At fust she thought he wur makin' fun,
So she laughed and said, ' Now, Sam, ha' done,
Thou needn't be tryin' it on wi' me,
Thou knaws I'd nivver think ill o' thee.
Thou's nivver had no 'casion for sayin' aught o' t'
kind.'
' Eneugh for thee to knaw,' says Sam, ' as I ha'
chaanged my mind.'

" Then Sally she wur downright mad—and sma'
blame too, says I—
She'd a spice o' temper, as lasses have as is smart
and neat and spry ;
' Thou ill-contrive't waistril, I wunder thou's th' face—
Thou knaws t' folk 'll cry thee shame thro'-out th'
hull o' t' place.
To talk sich stuff as that to her thou's walked out
wi' so long ;
Thou'dst better chaange thy mind agen, for sewer
thou's chaanged it wrong.'

" Hey, she gev' him a tung-lashin', a regilar set-down.
But Sam wur nivver daunted by any woman's frown ;
He let her talk till she wur tired, and then, ' My lass,'
says he,
' I've tauld thee as I've chaanged my mind, and that's
eneugh for thee.'

" Now, Sally she begun to see as tantrums wouldn't do ;
So next she tried clandoodlin'—and well she did it,
    too.
(I fun' it out at sivventeen, and I'll say 't at nigh
    three-score,
When a woman tak's to clandoodlin', a man may as
    well gi'e o'er.)
'Nay, Sam, thou nivver means it,' says she, and
    drops a tear ;
'We two ha' luvved each other for well-nigh sivven
    year,
An' we broke t' lucky sixpence, and vowed we'd
    nivver part ;
I nivver thought as thou wouldst go and try to
    break my heart !
An' if thou goes and leaves me now I'll lay me down
    and dee.'
I'm soft as a boiled turnip if a lass but wets her e'e,
But Sam he didn't care a smite, he wurn't that mak'
    o' stuff—
' I've chaanged my mind, I tell thee,' says he, ' and
    that's eneugh.'

" Now when clandoodlin' failed her, she knaw'd what
    to be at,
She went and tuk to strathegy—and woman's good
    at that.

I'm stronger nor th' missis, and wiser too, no
    doubt ;
But when she taks to strathegy, she beats me out
    and out.

      " Sally dreed her e'en, and smoothed her hair ;
      And med' believe as she didn't care.
        ' Well, Sam,' says she,
        ' It's nowt to me,
      I'm thinkin' there's plenty o' fish i' th' sea ;
      But what dosta think folk 'll say o' thee ?
      Now tho' thou'rt as bad a lot as can be,
      And hast seemin'ly lost all thy luv for me,
      I can't forget as I onc't luvved thee ;
      So I've a plan, an' if thou'll agree,
      Th' blame on t' partin' shall fall on me—
'Twould nivver do for a likely lad to leave a lass i'
    the lurch.
Thou mun go and see t' parson, and hav' us asked i'
    church ;
An' thou mun nivver cheep a word o' all as thou hast
    said,
An' things 'll go on just as tho' we still were boun' to
    wed.

" ' An' then t' parson he'll begin to tie us up for
    life,

" Sam, wilta ha' this woman to be thy wedded
　　wife,
To luv' an' keep an' cherish her thro' good report and
　　ill ? "
And thou mun then, as bauld as brass, mak' answer
　　" Ay, I will."
And then 'twill be my turn, thou knaws, an' he'll cum
　　to me and say,
" Sally, wilta ha' this man, to honour and obey ? "
And I shall toss my head as tho' I luvved thee ne'er
　　a jot,
And say out loud afore folk, " Nay, maister, I will
　　not."
　　　　　So then wi' me
　　　　　The fault will be,
　　　And none o' t' blame will lig o' thee.'

" Now Sam he thought 'twur just as well as she
　　should ha' th' blame,
So long as he could get his way, and leave her all th'
　　same.
So he went and put th' axins up, and when th' day
　　cum round,
A luvvinger couple, you'd ha' said, there couldn't well
　　be found.
And Sally wur that snod and smart, in ribbins and in
　　lace,

Wi' a smile as looked like mischief upon her bonny
  face ;
And her posy wur forget-me-nots, as might ha' been
  a hint—
But bless you, Sam he'd no more *nous* nor if he'd
  bin a flint.

" But he'd getten t' lesson off by heart, an' when t'
  parson said,
' Sam, wilta ha' this woman as thou's cum here to
  wed ? '
He wurn't nivver a bit flustered, tho' he'd behaved so
  ill,
But spoke out bauldly like a man, ' Ay, maister,
  that I will.'
And then a light o' triumph shone in Sally's e'en so
  blue,
And when t' parson speared at her, she answered,
  ' I will,' too.
' Hey, Sally, lass ! ' cried Sam, aghast, ' thou'st bin
  and clean forgot,
Thou *knaws* thou tauld me thou would say, ' Why,
  no, that I will not.'
' Hey, Sam, my lad, I knaw I did—but now, I think
  thou'lt find
It's quite eneugh for *thee* to knaw as *I* ha'
  CHAANGED MY MIND.' "

But Brimmacum didn't change his mind, and Aunt
    Lucy said, " I will ";
And Joe declared, " In twenty year happen she'll say
    it still ! "
And wasn't the cake just scrumptious ! Trust me,
    for you know I've tried,
And I shouldn't much mind a wedding myself, if
    they'd only leave out the bride !

PICKLED COCKLES :

A QUAKER STORY.

In the old-fashioned "Friendly" days,
When Quaker garb and Quaker ways
Had not died out—when Quaker phrase
Was heard in every Friendly greeting,
And not merely reserved for "Preparative Meeting:"
When old and young
Used the Quaker tongue,
Said "thee" and "thou,"
Declined to bow,
And thought a song
Most improper and wrong ;
In the days which we love—to hear about
(They were less amusing to live in, no doubt),
There dwelt just outside a suburban town
A dear old Friend named Tabitha Brown.

Now Tabitha Brown was clad always
In the softest of drabs and most dove-like greys ;

With the whitest of caps on her silver hair,
And apron and mittens and all "to compare ; "
While out of doors she was just the same,—
Most spotless, quiet, and free from blame ;
Her shawl was neatly folded in,
And kept in its place by a white-headed pin;
The sweet placid face, 'neath the silver hair
(Showing lines of sorrow, but none of care),
Looked out from a bonnet quaint and shady,—
She was what one might call a real " Quaker Lady."
Thy excuse, gentle spirit—I apprehend
Thou wert what's better still, a true " Woman Friend."

Tabitha Brown was well skilled in the arts
Of making pies, and puddings, and tarts;
Of pickling, preserving, and baking, and brewing,
Of boiling and roasting, and frying and stewing,
      Cheese-pressing and churning—
      In all sorts of learning
Connected with thrifty household ways,
Tabitha Brown was above all praise.
In fact, there was nothing she couldn't make,
From a whole-meal loaf to a wedding cake !

      While for dusting and rubbing,
      And scouring and scrubbing,
And subjecting all things to the process called
    " tubbing,"

For swilling and mopping, for sweeping with brooms,
For turning the furniture out of the rooms,
For shaking of beds and for beating of chairs,
For taking up carpets and cleaning the stairs ;
For polishing pots, pans, dishes, and kettles,
And everything else that is made of bright metals ;
For leaving black beetles and spiders no peace,
For using that article termed " elbow-grease,"
Together with soap, sand, bath-brick, and black-lead,
Emery paper (or what was then used instead),
For keeping the house without spot, speck, or stain,
There never was servant like Phœbe Jane !
In short, and most boys will, I think, grasp my
    meaning,
She kept up *all the year* one perpetual "spring-
    cleaning."

Phœbe Jane was tidy and trim,
But no Quaker dress could make her look prim ;
And, notwithstanding her " Friendly " gown,
She failed to resemble Tabitha Brown.
Her bonnet and shawl were just as plain,
Yet they looked somehow different on Phœbe Jane ;
While rebellious curls would sometimes stray
From her cap in a most unorthodox way,
And, though she persistently brushed them o'er,
They only curled tighter than before.

Her temper, too, was none of the best ;
And if any one, either mistress or guest.
Her peculiar notions chanced to offend, she
      Her feelings expressed
      (It must be confessed)
In Quakerly speech which was not always "friendly " ;
And Tabitha Brown wrote these words in her diary :
" P. J.'s heart—it is good, but her temper—is fiery."

This quiet household contained a third,—
A jackdaw, a really remarkable bird !
From the day he left his parental nest
In Quaker language he'd been addressed ;
And he talked in quite as " Friendly" a strain
As Tabitha Brown or Phœbe Jane.
      No schoolboy's freak
      Had e'er taught him to speak
Of "awfully jolly " or "stunning," or " fine,"
      Or to whistle sad airs
      About "oysters " and "stairs,"
And "Ehren," or "Bingen," or "Bonn " "on the
    Rhine."
      Sedate and grave,
      He knew how to behave ;
On points of decorum his feelings were sensitive ;
      Friends scarce had erred
      Had they sent this bird

To the " Quarterly Meeting " as " Representative."
Tho' no doubt he would not have failed to declare
That he certainly " did not expect to be there."

But not even beneficent Quaker law
Can eradicate mischief from a jackdaw,
  And a failing bad
  He once had had,
Which is common to all of his species and genus
(Pray let it be kept a secret between us)—
He had not a conscience sufficiently fine
To discriminate clearly 'twixt " mine " and " thine."
  On thimbles and keys,
  Button-hooks and green peas,
  Spoons (" tables " or " teas ")
  He would suddenly seize
  Without saying " please,"
And convey them to places not reached with great
 ease—
  To the tops of tall trees,
  Rocked by Spring's " gentle breeze."
Or to crannies thro' which your hand could not squeeze.
  Once, when many degrees
  Of cold made it freeze,
And Tabitha Brown 'gan to cough and to sneeze,
She sent for her doctor, the best of M.D.'s,
And this model jackdaw ran away with the fees.

But 'twas long ago
Since he'd acted so ;
And Tabitha gently said, " Thee know,
We ought to have charity, Phœbe Jane ;
I do not think 'twill occur again."

Now of all the receipts which Friend Brown possessed,
She prized one more highly than the rest,
Which, from mother to daughter handed down,
Had for years belonged to the race of Brown ;
'Twas for pickled cockles, and Friends would
    declare,
When they tasted the " Monthly Meeting " fare,
That this dish indeed was beyond compare.
So, though Tabitha looked with benignant eyes
On the rapid consumption of puddings and pies,
And showed, indeed, very small reserve
In the matter of marmalade and preserve,
She was somewhat "exercised in her mind,"
On entering the storeroom one morning, to find
That the jar she had thought was filled to the brim
With dainty molluscs in orderly trim,
Was in truth half empty ; and in some pain
She mentioned the fact to Phœbe Jane :
" They'll not last until cockles come round again."
But Phœbe Jane was very cross,
And, as she gave her head a toss,

Replied, " I thought thee couldn't know
That the stock was getting low
              ˙Of pickled cockles."

Tabitha quietly withdrew,
Yet still, alas! 'tis very true
That neither mistress nor maid could guess
How day by day the store grew less,
              Of pickled cockles.

And Phœbe Jane took it into her head
That her mistress didn't believe what she said,
And remarked, as she took the breakfast up,
" I know thee think that I dine and sup
              On pickled cockles."

And, though Tabitha calmly assured her that she
Had not the least doubt of her honesty,
Phœbe still declared that she couldn't remain
If her character wasn't freed from the stain
              Of those pickled cockles.

One afternoon it chanced that she
Was filling the little brass kettle for tea ;
When, turning round, with surprise she saw,
On the ground beside her, the grave jackdaw
              Eating pickled cockles.

The kettle falls, the waters pour
Over jackdaw, grate, and kitchen floor ;
And Phœbe cries, with excited feeling,
" Ah ! Friend, I see that thee've been stealing
                    The pickled cockles ! "

The poor jackdaw became very bald   ·
From the dire effects of that terrible scald ;
He looked a most deplorable fright,
And he never after could bear the sight
                    Of pickled cockles.

For a year and a day this poor little bird
Never opened his mouth to speak a word ;
At the end of that time an event occurred
Which caused his voice once more to be heard.
Tabitha Brown had a brother-in-law,
As strict a Quaker as ever you saw ;
His coat was long, and his collar was straight ;
You knew him at once as a " Friend of weight."
He wore a broad-brimmed beaver hat,
And rejoiced in the name of " Nathaniel Pratt."

          Now this " weighty Friend "
          Came up to attend
The famed " Yearly Meeting " of which you have
    heard,

Which begins, so Friends say,
" On the first Fourth day
Which follows the First day, in order the third,
Of the Fifth month."—Pray,
Might I venture to say
That this is rather a roundabout way
Of describing the third or fourth Wednesday in
May ?

'Twas First day morning, and eight or nine
Most " well-concerned Friends " had met to dine
At Tabitha Brown's. Nathaniel Pratt,
Who on the right hand of the hostess sat,
Still wore, sedately, his broad-brimmed hat ;
But having thus borne his testimony
In a manner in which he stood quite alone, he
Began to think that he now was free
To consider himself at liberty
To consult his comfort in some degree ;
So he took off his hat, and exposed to view
A massive head, which, I assure you,
Might have served as a model for Giunta, of Pisa,
Who loved to paint
A benevolent saint
As bald—as bald as Julius Cæsar,
With a halo instead of the laurel rare
Which the Senate permitted the latter to wear

To conceal the scarcity of his hair!
(For further particulars see Lemprière.)
The jackdaw, whom nobody thought of heeding,
Took a lively interest in the proceeding ;
And though he had never studied geology,
And had no acquaintance with natural laws,
It was plain to this cleverest of jackdaws,
That effect, as a rule, must proceed from cause.
Then, not stopping to make the slightest apology,
    . With a knowing air
    He perched on the chair
Of the " weighty Friend " who had lost his hair,
    And exclaimed in his ear
    In tones loud and clear,
But yet with a touch of pity sincere
(Inspired, no doubt, by a fellow feeling),
" *Ah, Friend ! I see that* THEE'VE *been stealing*
        The pickled cockles."

MORAL.

Don't steal Pickled Cockles—fresh ones are not dear
And if in your mind you are not quite clear
Concerning the pickling, look out the receipt on
Page three-ninety-one of the late Mrs. Beeton.
Thirdly, and lastly—I speak with due cause—
I should certainly strongly advise you to pause
Before you put faith in the best of Jackdaws!

THE QUAKER AND THE FAIRY.

Do you wonder at my title ?
Wonder at the strange conjunction
Of such widely different beings
(Different as drab from scarlet)
As a Quaker and a Fairy ?
Listen, then, and I will tell you,
Tell you all the wondrous story
Of an excellent young Quaker,
Much respected in his Meeting
By the name of Joseph Woodfall.

Drab his coat, and drab his gaiters,
And of buttons they were guiltless ;
And his hat was made of beaver,
And its brim was of the broadest.
Plain his dress and plain his speech was,
Few his words, but very weighty.
And he never read a novel,
Never read a work of fiction ;
But he studied Fox's journal,

And the works of Penn and Barclay ;
That was where he found amusement ;
Not in theatres or dancing,
Not in hunting or in rowing ;
Bicycles were not invented,
If they *had* been he would not have.
Wasted time in vain diversion ;
And he always went to Meeting,
Twice on First day, once on Fourth day,
Never thought a walk more pleasant.
Never said he had a headache,
Or his cold was very serious !
Clerk he was to Monthly Meeting,
Door-keeper at the Yearly ;
All the meetings he attended !

Now this excellent young Quaker
Fell in love with fair Priscilla—
Fairest maid in all the Meeting !
And he thought, if way would open
He would marry fair Priscilla.

Many virtues had Priscilla,
She was modest, neat, and tidy,
Soft her voice, and sweet her temper ;
And in all her household duties
None could equal fair Priscilla.

So he spoke unto the maiden,
Spoke with serious words and weighty.
Said he saw *his* duty clearly;
Hoped that well she would consider
And the same conclusion come to.
Thus he wooed her, thus he won her;
For our Quaker youths and maidens
Have hearts very much like others!
And the serious words of Joseph
Spoke a love as true and tender
As the sonnets of a poet!
And Priscilla's modest answer,
" Yea, I *think* I love thee, Joseph,"
Meant as much as love-lorn maiden
Ever sang to knight of story!

But, alas, no one is perfect!
Faults belong to human nature;
And Friend Joseph soon discovered
What he thought a serious failing
In the maid he loved so dearly.
Too light-hearted was the maiden—
Light her heart, and light her footstep,
And her merry, ringing laughter
Vexed the quiet soul of Joseph;
For he thought it was not seemly
To be very glad and joyous

In this world of sin and sorrow.
And she loved poetic stories,
Loved the " Faërie Queene " of Spenser,
And the bright and fair creations
Of sweet Shakespeare's wondrous pencil.
Found glad beauties in the sunshine,
In the flowers and sparkling dewdrops,
Which, to honest Joseph's notions,
Were but vain and idle fancies.
And she half believed in Fairies ;
Told him many a tale of wonder,
And the while he listened to her—
Listened, puzzled, yet enchanted—
Thoughts quite sober rose within him :
Would the habit of truth-telling
Not be injured by these stories?
Could her " yea " and " nay " be sacred
If she meddled with these fictions?
Would her wild imagination
Lead astray the sweet Priscilla?

But, one evening, while he pondered,
Much perplexed and puzzled sorely,
While he wondered if his duty
Bade him leave his fair Priscilla
(After words of kindly counsel),
Bade him lead a life most lonely,

Or seek out another woman
Not so fanciful or comely ;
While he pondered, puzzled sorely,
Suddenly, adown a moonbeam,
Gleaming through the open casement,
Came a little tiny creature,
Fairer than the loveliest mortal !
Blue her eyes as heaven's azure,
Golden hair fell o'er her shoulders ;
Dainty robes, of brightest colours,
Draped her little dancing figure.
She was just the sweetest Fairy
Human eyes have ever gazed on !
So this little graceful being,
Fluttering wings of gauzy silver,
'Lighted, gently as a roseleaf,
On the outspread hand of Joseph.
And, in tones of bell-like sweetness,
Said : " O unbelieving mortal,
I have come to teach thee wisdom.
Dost thou fear that Fairy legends
Will affect the truth of woman ?
Fairy tales are always truthful ;
Deep within them lies a meaning,
Meaning mystic, pure, and holy.
Only innocence can read it,
Only childhood in its freshness,

Only guileless men and women.
Thou art guileless, O Friend Joseph!
But, I fear, thou'rt rather stupid!
Yet, because thy heart is honest,
And because thy tongue is truthful
(Virtue most beloved of Fairies),
I have come to teach thee wisdom.
Come with me, and I will show thee
Something of this mystic meaning,
Something of the works of fancy!"

Honest Joseph, looking downwards
At the little graceful being,
At the sweetest of the Fairies,
Said: " I think 'tis not consistent
For a man Friend, staid and serious,
To be seen with one so flighty!
Is it seemly for a woman
To be seen with hair unloosened?
With a gown of gaudy colours,
And with jewels vain and sparkling?
Cover up thy wandering tresses
With a modest cap of muslin;
Change thy robe of flaring colours
For a gown more neat and simple;
Then, perchance, when thou returnest,
I will listen to thy teaching,

Try to find the mystic meaning—
Though, I fear me, weighty wisdom
Dwelleth not with one so flighty."

Then the Fairy's merry laughter
Followed Joseph's admonition,
And, without a word, she vanished.
In her place there stood a figure,
Clothed in garb of Quaker fashion ;
And the face was grave and serious,
And the bright blue eyes were downcast,
And the golden hair was gathered
Underneath a cap of muslin !
Slyly smiled she at his wonder,
But in modest tone she queried,
" Will I suit thee now, Friend Joseph ? "
Joseph answered, gravely, slowly,
" Verily, thou art more seemly ;
I will follow where thou leadest."

Out into the moonlight dancing
Went the little Quaker Fairy !
Honest Joseph followed after,
Pondering deeply, puzzled sorely.
Then she showed him sights of wonder ;
Nothing new she showed unto him,
But her wand gave brighter colours

To the glorious works of Nature,
And he saw a fairer beauty
In the sparkling of the dewdrops,
In the gleaming of the moonbeams,
In the bright and varied colours
Of the flowerets in the meadow.
Then he heard a sweeter music
In the splashing of the fountain,
In the ripple of the streamlet,
In the song of lark and linnet.
And the sound of human laughter,
And the songs of human gladness,
Seemed no longer sad and sinful.
Then she showed him human sorrow,
Comforted by sweetest fancy;
Memories of happy childhood,
Hopes of brighter days in future,
Raising men from weary sadness
To a cheerful, bright contentment;
Gilding many a dreary garret,
Soothing many a lonely pillow,
Bright'ning life in every dwelling.

Then she turned and spoke unto him:
"Fear not for thy wife Priscilla,
Wife she will be, for I know it.
Sorrow is the lot of all men,

Do not seek it ere it cometh.
Do not check her gladsome spirit,
Happiness is right, not sinful.
Let her listen to the poets,
Let her tell thee tales of wonder,
She will lead thy sober reason
To the brighter realms of fancy ;
And her wild imagination
Will be sobered by thy judgment.
Ye are suited to each other ! "

Then the Fairy vanished slowly !
And the excellent young Quaker
Woke from out his wondrous slumber.
From that day a change came o'er him ;
Still his hat was made of beaver,
Still its brim was of the broadest,
Still his speech was plain and friendly,
Still he studied Fox and Barclay,
Still he was a good young Quaker ;
But he listened to Priscilla,
Listened to her pretty fancies,
Did not check her joyous spirits ;
Nay, he sometimes smiled to see them.
So he married fair Priscilla,
And, in words of good old story,
" They lived happy ever after."

A ROMANCE OF A FRIEND'S BONNET.

" Unless Virtue guide us, our Choice must be wrong."
PENN'S " Maxims," 256.

ONE First day morn, I ween,
At " Meeting " might be seen,
  At the end
Of a sober boyish row,
On a form made short and low,
  A small " Friend,"

Feeling very new and strange,
Looking round him for a change
  To employ
His thoughts, which wandered free,
For he was, as all might see,
  A new boy.

But a short space did divide
The men's from the women's side,
  And near him,

Also at the short form's end,
Sat a little " Woman Friend "
   Neat and prim.

Her gentle, serious face
Seemed to suit the time and place ;
   Yet he tried
To compose his thoughts in vain,
They wandered off again
   To her side !

On the form, before each young
Woman Friend, a bonnet hung,
   Do not smile !
Covered each in dove-like hue ;
Fashioned plainly in the true
   Quaker style.

These bonnets, he did find,
With copy-books were lined,
   And he then
On each neatly-written page
Read the maxims grave and sage,
   Of Friend Penn.

And the bonnet, which he deemed
To the little maiden seemed
   To belong,

Spoke thus, with silent voice :
" Unless Virtue guide, our Choice
          Must be wrong."

'Twas " Second Meeting" day,
And the girls had gone away
          In grave state ;
And the boy then turned to heed
The words the Clerk did read,
          With due weight.

'Twas Query number three,
Which the Clerk read solemnly
          Up above.
" Do Friends," the boy preferred
To translate what he heard,
          " Fall in love ?" *

And in his childish mind
He an answer seemed to find
          Full and true ;
" To the best of our belief,"
Ran the wording, quaint and brief,
          " Yes, they do."

---

* III. Query. " Are Friends preserved in love one towards
another ; if differences arise, is due care taken speedily to end them ;
and are Friends careful to avoid) and discourage tale bearing and
detraction ? "—RULES OF DISCIPLINE.

Boy and girl grew youth and maid,
Trained beneath the firm and staid
   Quaker rule ;
Their paths ran side by side
For a time, then severed wide,—
   They left school.

The young man went astray
From the good old-fashioned way
   Of his youth ;
His collar was turned down,
His hat, from brim to crown,
   Changed, in sooth !

His bow had quite a grace,
And " Sunday " took the place
   Of " First day ";
He called " Seventh month," " July,"
And " business Meetings," "dry,"
   Sad to say !

Light literature he read ;
He learned to dance ('tis said).
   When he penned
His letters ('twas a blot)
He wrote, " Dear Sir," and not
   " Esteemed Friend."

     6

Yet still the maiden's face,
And her simple Quaker grace,
      In his heart,
With the words of love and truth
Which he learned in early youth,
      Had a part :

And oft, when doubts assailed
And temptation half prevailed,
      " Yet be strong,"
Cried memory's warning voice,
" Unless Virtue guide, our Choice
      Must be wrong."

Though his behaviour shocks
Friends of views orthodox,
      And minds deeper ;
At " Yearly-Meeting" he
By appointment came to be
      A doorkeeper.

" Would the present be the time
To receive Rebecca Pryme,
      We would learn,
And another Woman Friend
Under, as we apprehend,
      A concern ? "

The young Woman Friend who bore
This message to the door,
  Where he stood,
Wore a bonnet, plain and prim,
And the sight seemed unto him
  Very good !

For beneath the " friendly " shade
Was the sweet face of the maid
  (Thus it proved)
Whom, that First day long ago,
When they sat in silent row
  He had loved !

On no very distant day,
When there seemed an " open way,"
  And he came
To her, and spoke his mind,
She too, he joyed to find,
  Felt the same.

Guided by Virtue's voice,
Bless'd was this young man's choice ;
  And the twain
In the Meeting-house once more
Where they sat in days of yore
  Met again.

The Friends assembled there
In the quiet waiting share
                    With the bride,
And the husband, soon to be,
Who are sitting silently,
                    Side by side.

Then he takes her by the hand,
And the two together stand,
                    Ent'ring life ;—
" Until our lives shall end,
Dear Friends, I take this Friend
                    For my wife ;

" With assistance from Above
I promise faith and love "
                    (Thus he saith)
" As befits the married state,
Till the Lord shall separate
                    Us by death.'

THE KING'S PUDDING.

'TWAS drawing near to happy Christmastide ;
A sound of chopping, mingled with the hum
Of merry voices, reached my ears.   The scent
Of plums and spices filled the frosty air
With a rich, balmy fragrance ; and my thoughts
Reverted to that pudding made of old
In Arthur's time.   'Tis thus the legend runs :—
Three pecks of barley meal the King obtained,
Some say he stole.   'Tis well for them the sword
Excalibur, that mystic, wondrous brand,
Is safe within the keeping of a maid,
The Lady of the Lake.—May shame alight
On those who dare, with false and slanderous
        tongues,
T'assail the honour of the blameless king !—
This meal King Arthur took, and with the aid
Of all his knights and Guinevere his queen
He made the pudding so renowned in song !

He rolled it out, then with a liberal hand
He placed therein a goodly store of plums
And that it might be rich, but not too rich,
Two lumps of fat (of suet or of lard,
We learn not which, enough to say 'twas fat)
He added, not by weight, and not by guess,
Such clumsy methods must perforce suffice
In these degenerate days. In Arthur's time
Love brightened all the common things of life,
And poetry was linked with every act,
However humble, and so Arthur used
A standard worthy of a knightly king.
Each lump was fashioned of the size and shape
Of the white dainty thumb of Guinevere!
Thus closed his task. Then Galahad arose
And brought the bag, of samite pure and white
As his own fame ; and Tristram tied the string
And placed the pudding in a mighty pot,
Which hissed and bubbled with triumphant glee
As though it knew the honour which it gained
In being chosen from the common herd
To boil a pudding fashioned by a king !
For hours the pudding boiled. Then Lancelot
Essayed to take it up—for in all feats
Requiring steady eye and skilful hand
Sir Lancelot of the Lake was ever first.
Around him gathered soon a brilliant throng,

Watching with bated breath the dexterous knight,
Who lodged the pudding safely on a dish,
And placed it deftly on the table round. ·
Then all the Court did eat, and praised the King,
Whose knowledge of the peaceful household arts
Was equal to his prowess in the field ;—
And what they could not eat, the careful Queen,
In loving competition with her lord,
Fried for their breakfast on the morrow morn.
Then Enid took her harp and sang the strain
Familiar to our ears from childhood's days :

> " *When good King Arthur ruled this land,*
>   *He was a goodly king !*
> *He took three pecks of barley meal,*
>   *To make a bag pudding !*
>
> " *A bag pudding the King did make,*
>   *And stuffed it full of plums ;*
> *And in it put two lumps of fat,*
>   *As big as my two thumbs !*
>
> " *The King and Queen did eat thereof,*
>   *And noblemen beside ;*
> *And what they could not eat that day*
>   *The Queen next morning fried !* "

She ended, and in deep prophetic voice
Grave Merlin spake : " Let future ages learn

A lesson from this pudding made in sport.—
Oh, English men and women of all time,
Deal out your Christmas cheer with bounteous
    hand,
But let not sinful waste decrease your store !
Whate'er your rank or age do not disdain
To stir the pudding for the Christmas board ;
So shall you follow the example set
By good King Arthur and his beauteous queen."

DOROTHY.

(*A TALE OF HADDON HALL.*)

~~~~~~~~~~~~~~~~

GAILY the lights are shining
  In stately Haddon Hall,—
For a bridal night must needs be bright,
  And merrily goes the ball ;
'Tis whispered another such wedding
  Will not be far to seek,
For a lovely pair are the daughters fair
  Of Vernon,—" King o' the Peak."

Oh, cool is the little chamber
  Adjoining the great ball-room,—
And no one wonders that Dolly
  Should rest in the partial gloom ;
And no one recks of the mighty love
  That holdeth her heart in thrall,
Of the tears that rise as she sadly cries,
  " Farewell to Haddon Hall ! "

She gently closes the portal
　　That leads from Haddon Hall,
And the stone stair faintly echoes
　　The sound of her light foot-fall ;
She passes the lighted windows,
　　And steals in the night away.—
'Tis the story of old—love versus gold,—
　　And love has won the day.

There lingers a young wood-cutter
　　In the glades near Haddon Hall :
Yet never a king of the forest
　　'Neath his axe need fear to fall :
He waiteth now in the darkness,
　　One hand holds his noble steed,
While the other is laid on his trusty blade :—
　　A knightly churl indeed !

A rustle of silken garments,
　　A glitter of jewels rare,
A gleam of gold 'neath the cloak's dark fold,
　　And Dolly is standing there ;—
One moment of hurried greeting,
　　He lifts her over the wall,—
And away they ride, that youth and his bride,—
　　The heiress of Haddon Hall.

　　　*　　*　　*　　*　　*　　*　　*

A knight and gentle lady
  Hold sway in Haddon Hall,
And children fair bless the happy pair
  And love is lord of all.—
And a ducal race shall proudly trace
  Its lofty pedigree,
Back thro' ages gone, to the brave Sir John
  And the Lady Dorothy.

     *   *   *   *   *   *   *

The ivy twines round the turrets
  Of stately Haddon Hall,
But Dolly's face, with its girlish grace,
  Still smiles from the old oak wall;
And youths and maidens whisper low
  Of love that can do and dare,
As they rest awhile near the ancient pile
  On Dorothy Vernon's stair.—

They say you are wronged, sweet Dolly,
  By this tale of Haddon Hall,
That the course of true love ran smoothly,
  And you never eloped at all;
For you were a model daughter,
  As dutiful as fair;
So you ne'er took flight, on that festal night,
  Adown that old stone stair.

For Sir John took the orthodox method
   Of winning the prize which he gained ;
And the needful consent of parents
   Was duly asked, and obtained ;
So he never stood in the darkness,
   While the lights gleamed bright at the ball,
Nor risked his life, to claim as his wife
   The heiress of Haddon Hall.—

It does not sound so romantic,
   But may be 'twas all for the best ;—
Yet the " peacock in pride " shows side by side
   With the boar of the Vernon crest ;
And the old stone stair still standeth,
   And the picture hangs on the wall,
To prove without fail the truth of my tale
   Of the heiress of Haddon Hall !

W. Speaight & Sons, Printers, Fetter Lane, London, E.C.

JAMES CLARKE & CO.'S BOOKS.

"THIS DO." Six Essays in Practice. By R. F. HORTON, M.A. "The Christian in Business," "The Christian in Public Life," "The Christian in the Home," "Christ in Art," "Christ in Literature," "The Christian and Amusement." Second Edition, cloth, 2s.

DAILY CHRONICLE: "*They are, for a marvel, truly* Christian *discourses.*"
SPEAKER: "*There is a sweet reasonableness about these vigorous and persuasive addresses which is very attractive; and yet no one can read the book without feeling that the preacher speaks with the authority of a man who has not merely thought for himself, but fought his way to his own conclusions.*"

QUEER STORIES FROM RUSSIA. By CAPEL CHERNILO. With Illustrations from Photographs. Price 3s. 6d.

THE DAILY TELEGRAPH: "*Some incidents of real life in the dominions of the Czar are cleverly depicted in a series of 'Queer Stories from Russia.' They deal to a great extent with the trials which await those unfortunate Muscovites who presume to break away from the Orthodox Church and join the increasing ranks of the Stundists, or Protestant Dissenters. It is hardly fair to call these stories merely 'queer;' some of them are deeply pathethic.*"

THE BISHOP AND THE CATERPILLAR (as Recited by Mr. BRANDRAM), and other Pieces. By MARY E. MANNERS. Dedicated by permission to LEWIS CARROL. Price 1s.

ROSEBUD SONGS. By T. CRAMPTON and other Composers. Illustrations by ERNOLD A. MASON. Price 1s.

ROSEBUD RHYMES. A Special Selection of Nursery and other Rhymes. Illustrated by *Rosebud* Artists: LOUIS WAIN, ERNOLD A. MASON, and others. Price 1s.

GLORIA PATRI: or, Our Talks About the Trinity. By JAMES M. WHITON, Ph.D., Author of "New Points to Old Texts," "Beyond the Shadow," &c. Price 3s. 6d.

NONCONFORMIST CHURCH BUILDINGS. By JAMES CUBITT. Price 2s. 6d.

SUNDAY-SCHOOL AND VILLAGE LIBRARIES. By THOMAS GREENWOOD, F.R.G.S. Hints on the Management of Village and Sunday-school Libraries, with Lists of Suitable Books. Price 1s. 6d.

SOME NOBLE SISTERS. By EDMUND LEE. Price 5s.

A MORNING MIST. By SARAH TYTLER. Price 5s.

GLADYS' VOW. By Mrs. G. S. REANEY, Author of "Our Daughters." Price 3s. 6d.

IN THE FAR COUNTRY: a Story for Boys. By ALBERT E. HOOPER. Illustrations by ERNOLD A. MASON. Price 3s. 6d.

ON THE THRESHOLD : Talks to Young Men. By Rev.
T. T. MUNGER. New Edition. Price 3s. 6d.

THE EVOLUTION OF CHRISTIANITY. By Rev. LYMAN
ABBOTT, D.D., successor to HENRY WARD BEECHER, and
Editor of *The Christian Union.* Price 4s.

THE CHURCH OF TO-MORROW. By W. J. DAWSON.
Crown 8vo, price 3s. 6d.

PLAIN TRUTHS FOR PLAIN PEOPLE. Notes of a Visit to
a Quaker Adult School. Price 1s.

SCHOOL HYMNS, FOR SCHOOLS AND MISSIONS. Compiled
by E. H. MAYO GUNN. Price, cloth limp, 3d.; cloth
boards, 6d. Edition with Music in preparation.

THE SUNDAY AFTERNOON SONG BOOK. Containing 137
Hymns for use at "Pleasant Sunday Afternoons" and other
Gatherings. Compiled by H. A. KENNEDY, of the Men's
Sunday Union, Stepney Meeting House. Cloth limp, 2d.

DUNDEE ADVERTISER: "*The social and practical side of religion, and the
bearing of Christianity on the character and conduct of the individual and of
society, are prominent features of the hymns.*"
LITERARY WORLD: "*To read these Sunday songs, to sing them, and to remem-
ber them, will be in itself an education for our sons of toil.*"
CHRISTIAN LEADER: "*A collection which men can be expected to sing with
perfect sincerity.*"

THE CHRIST OF THE HEART, AND OTHER SERMONS.
By Z. MATHER, of Barmouth, Author of "The Inspired Book
and the Perfect Man." Crown 8vo, cloth, 5s.

THE EPIC OF THE INNER LIFE, BEING THE BOOK OF JOB
Translated Anew, and Accompanied with Notes and an Introduction Study. By JOHN F. GENUNG. Price 4s. net.

SERVICE IN THREE CITIES. Twenty-five years' Christian
Ministry. By S. PEARSON, M.A. Price 2s. 6d.

A POPULAR ARGUMENT FOR THE UNITY OF ISAIAH.
With an Examination of the Opinions of Canons Cheyne and
Driver, Dr. Delitzsch, the Rev. G. A. Smith, and others. By
JOHN KENNEDY, M.A., D.D. Price 2s. 6d.

WHO WROTE THE BIBLE? A Book for the People. By
WASHINGTON GLADDEN. Price 4s.

SPEAKER: "*The work of Dr. Washington Gladden is well named 'a book for
the people.' It fulfils its promise ; it is simple, untechnical, careful without being
erudite. It is a reverent book, too ; a man who believes the Bible to be inspired
and the Word of God, here explains how it has been handled by modern criticism
and with what results. For an intelligent reader interested in these questions
and wanting a survey of the whole field, it would be hard to find a more suitable
book.*"
BAPTIST: "*It is the clearest and amplest popular statement of the points in
dispute with which we are acquainted.*"

INSPIRATION AND INERRANCY. By C. A. BRIGGS, D.D.,
LLEWELLYN J. EVANS, D.D., HENRY PRESERVED SMITH,
D.D. With an Introduction by ALEXANDER BALMAIN
BRUCE, D.D. Price 3s. 6d.

MEMOIR OF AND SERMONS by the late Dr. STEVENSON, Brixton. Price 3s. 6d.

SCOTTISH LEADER : *"The book will be liked wherever it is read."*

GLASGOW HERALD : *"Sure of an affectionate reception from all Dr. Stevenson's friends."*

BRADFORD OBSERVER: *"Are all too brief. Much more might have been told to advantage concerning him. Notices of his work will be read with affectionate interest by his numerous friends and admirers."*

LOYALTY TO CHRIST. By JOHN PULSFORD, D.D. 7s. 6d.

THE RIGHT AND WRONG USES OF THE BIBLE. New Edition. By R. HEBER NEWTON, Rector of All Souls' Church, New York. Crown 8vo, cloth, 3s. 6d.

THYSELF AND OTHERS. Six Chapters on Practical Christianity. By Rev. SAMUEL PEARSON, M.A., formerly Minister of Highbury Quadrant Church. Cloth 16mo, 1s.

NEW POINTS TO OLD TEXTS. By Rev. JAMES M. WHITON, Ph.D., Author of "Gloria Patri," "Summer Sermons," "The Law of Liberty," &c., &c. Crown 8vo, cloth, 3s. 6d.

BURNING QUESTIONS. By WASHINGTON GLADDEN, D.D., Author of "Things New and Old." Second Edition. Crown 8vo, cloth, 3s. 6d.

THE FREEDOM OF FAITH. By Rev. T. T. MUNGER. Sixth Edition. Crown 8vo, 3s. 6d.

EARLY PUPILS OF THE SPIRIT. By JAMES M. WHITON, Ph.D. Crown 8vo, paper, 6d.

WHAT OF SAMUEL? By JAMES M. WHITON, Ph.D. Crown 8vo, paper cover, 1s.

BEYOND THE SHADOW. By JAMES M. WHITON, Ph.D. Third Thousand. Crown 8vo, cloth, 3s. 6d.

SCIENCE AND THE SPIRITUAL. By Prof. A. J. DU BOIS. Author of "Science and the Supernatural." Sewed, 6d.

HENRY WARD BEECHER IN ENGLAND : A MEMORIAL VOLUME. Consisting of SERMONS, PRAYERS, LECTURES, and ADDRESSES, together with A BIOGRAPHICAL SKETCH and PHOTOGRAPHIC PORTRAIT. Crown 8vo, cloth, 5s.

HENRY WARD BEECHER'S PRAYERS IN THE CONGREGATION. Crown 8vo, 4s. 6d.

HENRY WARD BEECHER'S LAST SERMONS. Sermons delivered at Plymouth Church after Mr. Beecher's return from England. Crown 8vo, cloth, 3s. 6d.

HENRY WARD BEECHER'S RELIGION AND DUTY. Fifty-Two Sunday Readings. Selected by Rev. J. REEVES BROWN. Crown 8vo, cloth, 3s. 6d.

THE SCRIPTURES, HEBREW AND CHRISTIAN. By EDWARD
T. BARTLETT, A.M., and JOHN P. PETERS, Ph.D. Complete
in Three Volumes. The Complete Edition now ready.

OUR PRINCIPLES. A CHURCH MANUAL FOR CONGREGA-
TIONALISTS. By Rev. G. B. JOHNSON. Fifth Edition. 6d.

AIDS TO PUBLIC PRAYER. By Rev. AMBROSE D.
SPONG. 6d.

GATHERINGS FROM THE WRITINGS OF THE LATE REV.
T. T. LYNCH. Crown 8vo, cloth, 2s. 6d. Second Series.

HISTORY OF THE FREE CHURCHES OF ENGLAND,
1688—1891. From the Reformation to 1851, by·HERBERT S.
SKEATS. With a Continuation to 1891, by CHAS. S. MIALL.
7s. 6d.

THE LATE REV. C. H. SPURGEON. A Fine Mezzotype
Portrait in Colours, with Autograph, reproduced by the London
Stereoscopic Company. Price ONE SHILLING AND SIXPENCE,
post paid, securely packed in Millboard Case; or framed in
handsome reeded black-and-gold, or brown-and-gold frame,
complete, packed in box, and forwarded carriage paid for 6s.

THE ART OF AUTHORSHIP: LITERARY REMINISCENCES,
METHODS OF WORK, AND ADVICE TO YOUNG BEGINNERS.
Personally contributed in illustration of the art of effective
written composition by the Leading Authors of the Day. Compiled and Edited by Rev. GEORGE BAINTON. Crown 8vo,
cloth, 5s.

ONE HUNDREDTH THOUSAND.

TASTY DISHES, Showing what we can have for Breakfast, Dinner, Tea, and Supper. Crown 8vo, 1s.

MORE TASTY DISHES. Price 1s. A Book of Tasty,
Economical, and Tested Recipes. Including a Section on
Invalid Cookery. A Supplement to "Tasty Dishes."

SALA'S JOURNAL: "*Admirably adapted for the needs of small households, as
well as for the special requirements of invalids.*"
PEARSON'S WEEKLY: "*Every recipe is so clearly stated that the most inexpe-
rienced cook could follow them and make dainty dishes at a small cost.*"
BRIGHTON GAZETTE: "*The recipes embrace the entire range of ordinary
cookery in cases of sickness and health, and they are all written out in the plainest
language. No home ought to be without this timely, useful, and practical family
friend.*"

A Wedding Present or Gift-Book to Young Married People.

THE HOME: IN ITS RELATION TO MAN AND TO SOCIETY.
By late Rev. JAMES BALDWIN BROWN. Crown 8vo, cloth,
3s. 6d. In handsome Calf or Morocco binding, 10s. 6d.

HOMELY TALKS ABOUT HOMELY THINGS. By MARIANNE
FARNINGHAM. Foolscap 8vo, cloth, 2s. 6d.

WHAT SHALL WE NAME IT? A Dictionary of
Baptismal Names for Children. Containing 2,000 names, with
their meaning and the countries from which they originated. 6d.

Poetry.

BY MARIANNE FARNINGHAM.

GILBERT AND OTHER POEMS. By MARIANNE FARN-INGHAM. Third Edition. Fcap. 8vo, extra cloth, 3s. 6d.; gilt edges, 4s.

LAYS AND LYRICS OF THE BLESSED LIFE. By MARIANNE FARNINGHAM. Eighth Thousand. Revised edition. Crown 8vo, cloth, 2s. 6d.; gilt edges, 3s.

LEAVES FROM ELIM : POEMS. By MARIANNE FARN-INGHAM. Third Thousand. Crown 8vo, cloth, 4s.; gilt edges, 4s. 6d.

SONGS OF SUNSHINE : The Newest Volume of Poems by MARIANNE FARNINGHAM. Second Thousand. Crown 8vo, cloth, 4s.

For Young People.

DIALOGUES FOR SCHOOL AND HOME. By Rev. H. J. HARVEY. A companion book to the "Reedham Dialogues." Imperial 32mo, cloth, 1s.

BOYHOOD : A COLLECTION OF FORTY PAPERS ON BOYS AND THEIR WAYS. By MARIANNE FARNINGHAM. Eighth Thousand. Fcap. 8vo, 1s. 6d.; gilt edges, 2s.

BYE-PATH MEADOW. By late Rev. E. PAXTON HOOD. Fcap. 8vo, cloth, 3s. 6d.

CHILDREN'S HOLIDAYS. By MARIANNE FARNINGHAM. 1s.

THE CLARENCE FAMILY; or, Brothers and Sisters. By MARIANNE FARNINGHAM. Fcap. 8vo, cloth, 1s. 6d.; gilt edges, 2s.

GIRLHOOD. By MARIANNE FARNINGHAM. Twentieth Thousand. Fcap. 8vo, cloth, 1s. 6d.; gilt edges, 2s.

HOME LIFE : TWENTY-NINE PAPERS ON FAMILY MATTERS. By MARIANNE FARNINGHAM. A Companion Volume to "Girlhood." Eighth Thousand. Fcap. 8vo, cloth, 1s. 6d.; gilt edges, 2s.

LITTLE TALES FOR LITTLE READERS. A Book for the Little Ones. By MARIANNE FARNINGHAM. Uniform with "Girlhood," "Boyhood," and "Home Life." Fcap. 8vo, cloth, 1s. 6d.; gilt edges, 2s.

THE MORAL PIRATES, AND THE CRUISE OF "THE GHOST." With TWENTY-FIVE ILLUSTRATIONS. By W. L. ALDEN. Crown 8vo, cloth, 2s. 6d.

REEDHAM DIALOGUES. A Dozen Dialogues for Children. By late JOHN EDMED, Head Master of the Asylum for Fatherless Children, Reedham, Croydon. Eighth Thousand. Imperial 32mo, cloth, 1s. 6d.

WHAT OF THE NIGHT? A Temperance Tale of the Times. By MARIANNE FARNINGHAM. Fourth Thousand. Crown 8vo, Illuminated Cover, 1s.

THE ROSEBUD ANNUAL FOR 1893. Nearly 300 Illustrations by LOUIS WAIN, ERNOLD A. MASON, A. T. ELWES, G. STODDART, J. A. SHEPHERD, HARRY DIXON, and other well-known Artists, and numerous Stories in Prose and Verse. Twelve Pieces of Music by T. CRAMPTON and other Composers. Printed on stout fine paper. Handsome cloth binding. 4s.

** " *The Rosebud Annual*" *is acknowledged on all hands to be the best possible gift-book for small children.* " *No nursery is complete without it.*"

One Volume Novels.

1900 ? a Forecast and a Story. By MARIANNE FARNINGHAM, Author of " The Cathedral Shadow," &c., &c. Price 3s. 6d. Crown 8vo, cloth.

FOR PITY'S SAKE, and THE LOST LEADER. By MARY LINSKILL. Being THE CHRISTIAN WORLD ANNUAL for 1892. Price 1s.

A MAN'S MISTAKE. By MINNIE WORBOISE. Crown 8vo, cloth, 5s.

ALL HE KNEW. A religious Novel. By JOHN HABBERTON, Author of " Helen's Babies," &c. Crown 8vo, cloth, 2s. 6d.

ROSLYN'S TRUST. By LUCY C. LILLIE, Author of " Prudence," " Kenyon's Wife," " The Household of Glen Holly." Crown 8vo, cloth, 3s. 6d.

FOR THE RIGHT : A GERMAN ROMANCE. By EMIL FRANZOS. Given in English by JULIE SUTTER (translator of " Letters from Hell"). Preface by Dr. GEORGE MACDONALD. Crown 8vo, cloth, 3s. 6d. Third Edition.

" *I have seldom, if ever, read a work of fiction that moved me with so much admiration.*"—GEORGE MACDONALD.

DINAH'S SON. By L. B. WALFORD. Crown 8vo, cloth, 3s. 6d.

HAGAR : A NORTH YORKSHIRE STORY. By MARY LINSKILL, Author of " Between the Heather and the Northern Sea," " The Haven under the Hill," &c., &c. Crown 8vo, 1s.

LILLO AND RUTH ; or, Aspirations. By HELEN HAYS. Crown 8vo, cloth, 3s. 6d.

MERTONSVILLE PARK; OR, HERBERT SEYMOUR'S CHOICE.
By Mrs. WOODWARD. Fifth Edition. Crown 8vo, cloth, 5s.

CLARISSA'S TANGLED WEB. By BEATRICE BRISTOWE.
Crown 8vo, cloth, 5s.

SISTER URSULA. By LUCY WARDEN BEARNE. Crown
8vo, cloth, 5s.

PRISCILLA; OR, THE STORY OF A BOY'S LOVE. By CLARA
L. WILLMETS. Cloth, 1s. 6d.

THE CATHEDRAL SHADOW. By MARIANNE FARN-
INGHAM. Fifth Thousand. Crown 8vo, cloth, 3s. 6d. ; gilt
edges, 4s.

THE SNOW QUEEN. By MAGGIE SYMINGTON. Third
Thousand. Fcap. 8vo, cloth, 1s. 6d. ; gilt edges, 2s.

BY AMELIA E. BARR.

*" Mrs. Barr's stories are always pleasant to read. They are full of sweetness
and light."*—SCOTSMAN.
*" In descriptive writing, in simplicity and gracefulness of style, and in perfect
mastery over her characters, Mrs. Barr can hold her own with any living English
novelist."*—GLASGOW HERALD.

A ROSE OF A HUNDRED LEAVES. By AMELIA E. BARR,
Author of "Jan Vedder's Wife," "Friend Olivia," &c. With
Numerous Illustrations. Printed on a superfine paper. Hand-
some cloth binding. 6s.

FRIEND OLIVIA. A Quaker Story of the Time of the
Commonwealth. By AMELIA E. BARR. Crown 8vo, cloth, 6s.

J. GREENLEAF WHITTIER, THE QUAKER POET, WHO HAS JUST DIED, WROTE
TO MRS. BARR: *" My Dear Friend,—But for failing health and sight, which
make even a brief note a painful effort, I should long ago have told thee how much
I admire thy FRIEND OLIVIA. I read it as it appeared in 'The Century,'
and marvelled at its admirable portraiture of the early Quakers and their times.
As a Quaker, I heartily thank thee for it. I shall read it again in book form,
though my eyes do not allow me to use them much. Let me tell thee that, though
I read but sparingly any new literary works, I have read every book of thine with
great interest. I congratulate thee on their great success, and am gratefully thy
sincere friend,—*JOHN G. WHITTIER."

In a variety of handsome cloth bindings, or bound uniformly, crown 8vo.

THREE SHILLINGS AND SIXPENCE EACH.

A SISTER TO ESAU	IN SPITE OF HIMSELF
SHE LOVED A SAILOR	A BORDER SHEPHERDESS
THE LAST OF THE MAC-	PAUL AND CHRISTINA
ALLISTERS	THE SQUIRE OF SANDAL SIDE
WOVEN OF LOVE AND GLORY	THE BOW OF ORANGE RIBBON
FEET OF CLAY (*with portrait*	BETWEEN TWO LOVES
of author)	A DAUGHTER OF FIFE
THE HOUSEHOLD OF McNEIL	JAN VEDDER'S WIFE

*** *A new and cheap edition of "*JAN VEDDER'S WIFE *" is now
issued. In paper cover, price 1s. 6d.*

THE HARVEST OF THE WIND, AND OTHER STORIES.
By AMELIA E. BARR. Crown 8vo, paper, 1s.

NOVELS BY EMMA JANE WORBOISE.

NEW AND CHEAP EDITION.

*** *These Novels, which have hitherto been sold at Five Shillings each, are now issued at*

THREE SHILLINGS AND SIXPENCE EACH.

THORNYCROFT HALL
MILLICENT KENDRICK
ST. BEETHA'S
VIOLET VAUGHAN
MARGARET TORRINGTON
THE FORTUNES OF CYRIL
  DENHAM
SINGLEHURST MANOR
OVERDALE
GREY AND GOLD
MR. MONTMORENCY'S
  MONEY
NOBLY BORN
CHRYSTABEL
CANONBURY HOLT
HUSBANDS AND WIVES
THE HOUSE OF BONDAGE
EMILIA'S INHERITANCE

FATHER FABIAN
OLIVER WESTWOOD
LADY CLARISSA
GREY HOUSE AT ENDLESTONE
ROBERT WREFORD'S DAUGH-
  TER
THE BRUDENELLS OF BRUDE
THE HEIRS OF ERRINGTON
JOAN CARISBROKE
A WOMAN'S PATIENCE
THE STORY OF PENELOPE
SISSIE
THE ABBEY MILL
WARLEIGH'S TRUST
ESTHER WYNNE
FORTUNE'S FAVOURITE
HIS NEXT OF KIN.

The following 3s. 6d. Volumes are now issued at Three Shillings each.

MARRIED LIFE ; OR, THE STORY OF PHILLIP AND EDITH.
OUR NEW HOUSE ; OR, KEEPING UP APPEARANCES.
HEARTSEASE IN THE FAMILY | AMY WILTON
MAUDE BOLINGBROKE | HELEN BURY

A limited number of the following Novels, published at FOUR SHILLINGS AND SIXPENCE, are now offered at TWO SHILLINGS AND SIXPENCE.

CAMPION COURT
EVELYN'S STORY
LOTTIE LONSDALE

SIR JULIAN'S WIFE
THE LILLINGSTONES
THE WIFE'S TRIALS

www.ingramcontent.com/pod-product-compliance
Lightning Source LLC
Chambersburg PA
CBHW032147010726
47493CB00008BA/2617